KEEAN MURRELL-SNAPE

Occult 24/7

For Kira, the keeper of my cold black heart.
Please don't forget to dust the jar and change its brine every so often.

Foreword

Occult 24/7 Mix Tape.

1. *Alive After Death* - John Carpenter
2. *Unsatisfied* - The Replacements
3. *A Forest* - The Cure
4. *Rooms on Fire* - Stevie Nicks
5. *Here Comes Your Man* - The Pixies
6. *Secret Loser* - Black Sabbath
7. *Girls Just Want to Have Fun* - Cyndi Lauper
8. *Wild Thing* - X
9. *Road House Blues* - The Jeff Healy Band
10. *She Drives Me Crazy* - Fine Young Cannibals
11. *The Look* - Roxette
12. *Cult of Personality* - MC5
13. *Everybody Wants to Rule the World* - Tears for Fears
14. *Spellbound* - Siouxsie & the Banshees
15. *Funky Cold Medina* - Tone-Loc
16. *She's Like the Wind* - Patrick Swayze ft Wendy Frazier
17. *Epic* - Faith No More
18. *Can't Hardly Wait* - The Replacements

Acknowledgments

Mr Luckhurst*, a terrible teacher, *Ear Movies* podcast producer and a perfectly adequate friend. Thanks for fixing stuff. Christopher Pike, the reason I started writing at all. Ma, thanks for telling the video store it was fine for me to rent *T2: Judgment Day* when I was not yet age MA15+ after I made them call you to check. John Carpenter, my soundtrack to everything from writing and D&D; to days I want to feel like a cool doing chores. G & M, for everything.

*Editor's note: *Doctor* Mr Luckhurst

1

Halloween 1889, 11:57 PM

The stately and grand library of Vass Manor was like something out of Edgar Allen Poe caught in a supernatural hurricane. Parchment swirled in flurries, hardcover volumes of forgotten lore flew from shelves like penny dreadfuls, lightning crackled and thunder roared.

Beneath the eye of the storm stood a black stone altar on a black marble floor inlaid with eight occult symbols. Their origin and veracity would have been thought arcane and dubious, if not for the storm and the fact that they glowed with ancient cosmic power. Each symbol was linked across the floor with a fine inlaid tendril of gold connecting them like the roots of a tree that climbed the heavy stone plinth to a ninth symbol on the altar itself.

Bracing themselves against this peculiar storm were men, a dozen masked and hooded figures. Members of a secret society, mere moments away from invoking a powerful entity from beyond our realm. An entity said to grant those who pleased it through ritual and deference untold power to shape the world. The final step of this ritual was a classic of the dark arts: the sacrificing of a virgin.

Unfortunately for all gathered…

Stephanie Munro was not a virgin.

Poor Stephanie. Only days ago she'd turned nineteen with unfulfilled dreams of marrying rich. She now lay dead on the altar with an ornate triangular ritual dagger sticking out of her pale white chest. The dagger was beautiful and terrible, with channels designed to deny gravity and funnel blood up and out of a hole in the end of its hilt.

Looming above her was the perpetually put upon face, despite his vast wealth and privilege, of Giles Alexander Vass IV. He scratched a violently red patch of dry skin on his balding head as he argued with his younger, dandified, hot Victorian daddy with a villain mustache brother, Augustus Alexander Vass III.

They pushed each other back and forth like children in a schoolyard scuffle, a private school for sure.

"YOU DEFILED OUR VIRGIN, GUS!" yelled Giles over the roar of the storm as he swung a limp hand to slap Augustus. Augustus was too quick for him. He coolly avoided the attack and in return jabbed his older brother on the nose, wheeling his fists like an amateur pugilist.

"DON'T GET HYSTERICAL, GILES. YOU'RE MAKING A SCENE!" he yelled back.

Giles was incensed. He was almost always incensed. Tonight it was earned.

"A SCENE!" he screamed as he pulled the dagger from Stephanie's chest and lunged at his brother with it. Augustus laughed before realizing Giles meant to do him actual harm.

Augustus ran around the altar, his brother chasing him. For those watching, it might have played as comedy if not for the terror of what was happening above them. Neither man was paying attention to the eye of the storm that now hovered and swirled above the altar below the library's fourteen-foot ceilings, where a single line of light had appeared. The line split as it ripped open the fabric of space-time to somewhere dark, to somewhere full of shadows and dread. If Giles and Augustus had bothered to look upon this darkness, they would have seen teeth. Giant human-like teeth organized in rows. Teeth inside the gigantic maw of the entity they had hoped to please. The tempest was joined by a great sucking wind which pulled all towards the rip, towards The Maw.

On the altar, from the wound in her chest, Stephanie Munro's blood spiraled upwards into the eye of the storm and entered the rip.

The Maw roared at the taste. Somehow in ways we poor, delicate, soft-bodied humans could never understand, it knew this was not the blood of a virgin. Furious, The Maw's rows of teeth began to spin, each in the opposite direction of its neighboring row like some cosmic flesh, bone and enamel washing machine of doom.

Around the room, the few remaining loyal Vass Occultists who had not already exited stage left now panicked and fled. One man daring to fight the terror he felt at the sight of The Maw crawled towards the altar to grab a heavy leather bound *grimoire* that had been knocked aside by Giles and Augustus' fighting. He only just escaped as the suction of The Maw's vortex of teeth increased.

Giles, still chasing Augustus, felt the dagger ripped from his grip, sucked away by the wind. Stephanie Munro's corpse lifted, her back arching from the altar, and she rose up through the rip and into The Maw's spinning teeth. What was once a promising young woman of good breeding instantly became a mist of blood and pulp. Most, but not all, of her was sucked into the dark beyond The Maw's teeth. What escaped spewed back out and into the circling storm, splattering Giles, who stood slack-jawed in awe. Some of the airborne chunky soup that had once been Stephanie Munro splattered into his mouth. He spat out what didn't slide down his throat, gagging as his feet left the ground. Reaching out, he grabbed the edge of the altar as his heels lifted above his head.

Augustus laughed at his brother, not noticing that he, too, was now rising towards The Maw. Scrambling, he grabbed Giles' left leg and halted his ascent.

"DAMN YOU, AUGUSTUS! LET GO! YOU'VE KILLED US!" Giles screamed.

"YOU ARE ALWAYS SO DRAMATIC, BROTHER. IT'S FINE. I'M SURE THE GREAT MAW WILL FORGIVE US IF WE JUST EXPLAIN. SHE CAME ONTO ME, BROTHER. I HAD NO CHOICE!" Augustus retorted.

An Occultist screamed as he whipped by them, suddenly silent as his head bounced off the altar with a thud. His body spun up through the rip and blitzed against The Maw's teeth.

"CHRIST. THAT DOES LOOK UNPLEASANT, DOESN'T IT, GILES?" said Augustus as Giles was hit again with a vicious red mist of what had previously been a person. Giles' eyes stung as he cried. His tears lifted from his cheeks to join the storm.

"OH, COME ON NOW. BUCK UP, SPORT," patronized Augustus.

Deep inside Giles, really deep, somewhere within the primate part of his brain, something snapped. The weight of thirty years of being the one who had suffered because of his brother's actions finally broke him. With deliberate thought and malice, he kicked his legs to shake Augustus off him and into The Maw.

The betrayal was clear. Augustus knew he might have gone too far, but still, how dare his brother be angry with him for his loins' desire? As if he had the right to deny his gift from the gods of a rapacious sexual appetite.

"YOU DID THAT ON PURPOSE! GILES PLEASE, I'M SORRY! THINK ABOUT OUR SONS!" he begged. He actually hated his sons, and he hated Giles' idiot brood even more.

Giles didn't hear him. He had already made a choice. Unable to extricate his brother from his leg and his life, he closed his eyes and took a deep breath. He could hear the sound of his pounding heart as it slowed. He was calm and resigned. He let go.

Giles and Augustus Vass were obliterated by The Maw, just like the others.

The stained glass roof of the library tore off as the storm blew it open. The rip in space-time extended vertically into the night sky like the inverted roots of a tree above the Victorian pile of Vass Manor. Blood and debris from the library fountained with explosive force, spreading over the grounds. Among the wreckage, the ornate ritual dagger slammed and stuck into the manor's neat hedge gardens. And then just as suddenly as it had appeared, the rip knitted itself back together like a wound. The storm evaporated to reveal billions of stars. The world was quiet again except for the distant sound of a grandfather clock chiming midnight, out of tune.

2

99 years, 364 days later

October 30 1989, 10:35 PM

The V-Mart 24/7 convenience store sat alone on a large lot on the edge of town. It was clean but slightly neglected. Business had never been the same since the bypass had been built five years back. Underwood had always been a drive-through town and now it was a drive-by town. Nothing ever happened there.

Sitting on the curb, slightly to the right of the front doors, was Audrey Mack. She rolled her black mascara-masked scary blue eyes so hard she almost passed out from the joy of it. She was sixteen, pocket sized with black bottle hair and a deliberate streak of gray just like Nancy from *A Nightmare on Elm Street,* her favorite movie. Her face was paler than a full moon. She lit a cigarette, taking a deep drag and exhaling swirling smoke in disbelief.

"You and *Annie Munro?* Not possible," she said to her best friend William Davoe, who was sitting next to her on the curb.

William, or Billy to most people and just B to Audrey (he called her A), drummed his black-on-black nail-polished fingers on his ripped black jeans to a rhythm only he could hear. If he was surprised or bothered by her lack of faith he didn't show it. B was six months older than A. He was one of the few Black kids in town. He ran his hands through his close cropped purple hair that A had dyed it for him, then pulled his two size too big thrift store-found black leather jacket tight and kept drumming. Sitting on the other side of Audrey was their other best friend, Courtney Vazquez. B wanted the three of them to start a band. None of them knew how to play instruments. B didn't think that was a problem.

"You and Annie Munro... it would shake the pillars of heaven, earth and hell," said Courtney misquoting from *Big Trouble in Little China*. It was well know to all of them that C thought Kurt Russell was a total babe.

Courtney, C to A and B, was taller than both of them. All soft curves. She was, in her own words, a Hispanic Glam Queen. She had big black hair and even bigger moods. A few weeks from turning seventeen, she rocked a Stevie Nicks t-shirt as she sucked on a 'Blood' flavored apple raspberry, Monster Sized Big Suck.

The Big Suck was the V-Mart's similar but legally distinct knockoff of 7-Eleven's Slurpee. They were almost identical except for the Big Suck's unexplained slightly medicinal after-taste that you got used to after sucking down a few hundred of them like Courtney and her friends had done over the years.

The three of them were Underwood's rare and glorious weirds and this was *their* curb. They had been friends since the dawn of time, sometime in the early seventies. None of them remembered meeting. They had just always been and always would be friends. Especially if A had anything to do with it.

They had found their curb about three years ago after a disastrous attempt to attend a high school party. Ten minutes in they'd had the collective realization that they hated everyone they went to school with, that beer tasted like stale ass and that what they really wanted was a Big Suck. That night they had claimed the curb as their own. So far no one had tried to fight them for it, to A's eternal bitter disappointment. A had never been in a fight, but conceptually she liked the idea of enjoying violence.

"Your face would melt off if Annie Munro even looked at you," A said to B, incredulously.

"Totally," said C. "What A said. The whole thing."

"You're wrong. She's rad. She has good records. We made out and listened to *Tim*," said B.

"You did not *Tim* with her. She would not *Tim*," A snorted.

In A's mind there was just no way Annie Munro, popular girl, cheerleader and fashion victim was into Minnesota's own The Replacements, let alone into B. She was too normal. He was too weird. Just like them.

Before B could answer that Annie did in fact dig *Tim*, The Mats' celebrated fourth studio album, C dropped her Big Suck and grabbed her head as almost terminal brain freeze instantly stopped all time and thought.

"I sucked too fast," she managed to get out as she rubbed her temples. Brain freeze was Courtney's only naturally occurring enemy along with Alex Trebek and felt. She dropped a Big Suck every second or third attempt at consumption.

"Beware the Big Suck," B mocked in the spooky voice of Count Suckula, the V-Mart's cheesy vampire mascot. At their feet, a dark red ice sludge now leaked out of the image of The

Count's head etched on the side of the sixty-nine ounce plastic Monster Big Suck cup. (The Monster was three more ounces than 7-Eleven's new Double Gulp, a fact The Count proclaimed proudly in a speech bubble on the cup.)

"Story of our lives," said A as she blew out a deliberately big cloud of smoke. A would never have taken Drama because people might 'see' her, but she was always dramatic. She had never met an anthill she didn't treat like a mountain she'd love to bleed out on the side of.

C smiled again as the pain in her brain-place slowly subsided. C loved these two weirds like she'd birthed them herself.

"Do you think Mrs K will spot me another one?" C asked.

"You know she will," said B.

"She's basically your Mom," said A.

"She totally wants you to marry Jonathan and have cute glam babies," said B.

"Twins. Stevie and Nicks," added A.

That sounded amazing to C. Jonathan was Mrs K's son. He was nineteen, in community college and a total babe. Maybe even more total than Kurt Russell, if that was even possible.

"He *is* a total babe and the totality is overwhelming," C said with heavy breath.

"You should ask J for a Big Suck," said A.

"Would you not?" fired back C.

"Yeah. I would. Wood," said A.

"I wood lumber too" said B.

They all laughed at how dumb their bullshit was. Some nights, all they had was wordplay and their shitty attitudes. It got them through though. They were all silent for a second. The only noise was the wind rustling through the nearby woods, the muffled sound of the TVs inside the V-Mart and the hum of traffic on the distant interstate.

A ruined it. That was her thing.

"Hey, what do you want to do for Halloween?" she asked.

"I don't know. It's bullshit it's a Tuesday. I have to be home by eleven," said C, crinkling her nose.

C's Mom and Dad were super protective of her since her Mom caught cancer last summer. She was was in remission now, but not yet in the clear. As a result, her parents treated C like she was the one who was sick and needed to be protected from germs, especially Audrey and Billy. Her dad would've wrapped her in cling wrap and locked her in a closet if he knew they were hanging out at the V-Mart and not at A's place like she had told them. Thankfully her Dad brought his beer and nuts from the 7-Eleven on the other side of town.

"Costumes! We can lurk and scare any normals that dare step foot on V-Mart property", she said, her eyes lighting up.

"Wouldn't that just be like every other Tuesday?" B was skeptical.

"And Wednesday," said C.

"And Thursday," said B.

"Yeah, yeah all the days."

A pushed B and he rolled with it, never stopping drumming.

"I want to do SOMETHING. Nothing ever happens here," A moaned. She was right. Underwood was dead after five pm every night of the week. Actually before five pm too, she realized.

"The bubblegum factory burnt down," said B.

"Yeah, yeah, we were nine and you lost your mind. The whole town smelt like Original," she said, rolling her eyes. Anytime she complained that nothing happened in Underwood, B would bring up the *Great Underwood Gum Fire of '82*, which she had to begrudgingly admit was certainly something that had happened. The factory had been the last relic of Underwood's industrial past. Now it was gone, most adults worked in the other bigger towns outside of the valley. No one had ever figured out what had caused the fire.

"I love gum. I like fire. It was a good time," B smiled cheekily.

"I'm going to ask Mrs K for another Suck. You want anything?" said C, standing up.

"I'm good," said B shaking his head and double timing his drumming.

"Say 'Hi' to Jonathan and buy me an old Coke," said A. New Coke was the absolute pits. For some reason, Mrs K stocked a ton of it. A had no interest in "*C-c-catching the wave,*" despite Max Headroom's insistence. Her parents had HBO, and she remembered when the show had been cool, back before Max became a corporate shill.

C nodded and walked inside the store.

A put her head on B's shoulder. He stopped drumming and gave her a little hug. A was prone to melancholy, and stuff like Halloween meant a lot to her. B knew she would absolutely get her way, and he was fine with that except for a growing feeling at the bottom of his stomach that he identified as nervousness from the idea of telling A he might want to hang out with Annie instead of them tomorrow night. If Annie asked him, that was. She probably wouldn't. She would probably be doing popular shit with popular people.

"I wish we lived somewhere where the leaves turned brown and died for Halloween," A said. Underwood didn't really have seasons. Magically, unknown to the three of them, it was because of *actual* magic. It meant that the weather never really dipped below seventy degrees despite being an inland town nestled in a valley surrounded by creepy ass woods full of overgrown owls you did not want to fuck with.

"Grim. I'm good with it being warm out," he said.

"You still sleeping with the Carpet King? You know you can crash at mine. Rich and Judy love you. They *prefer* you. You talk to them," she said.

A's parents Rich and Judy were great. A hated them. They were both too involved and desperately wanted to be cool with whatever Audrey wanted to do. They were Democrats and needed everyone to know that they did not vote for George Bush or Ronald Reagan.

"The King and I are on good terms. Best to stay out of the Major's way till the sun is up and he's sleeping."

B's dad was ex-army and all hard ass with a heart of gold. Both B's parents worked alternating swing shifts and sometimes doubles at the VCR plant in Brookvale, two towns out of the valley and across the river. It meant B had to be as quiet as a mouse coming and going or take another serve of tough love and a rant about the value of discipline. B had taken to finding other places to sleep to keep out of his Dad's way. His mother was too tired to stand up for him, but always made sure he had dinner waiting in the icebox. Even if it was just frozen pizza rolls. At sixteen and a half, he was counting the days until he could move out. Where and how he'd pay rent were future B's problems. Meanwhile, the Carpet King was easy to live with and rent free.

Inside the V-Mart, the new video for *Here Comes Your Man* by The Pixies was playing on the store's TVs as C pulled the 'Blood' handle on the Big Suck machine. Sugary frozen apple raspberry goo splattered out and filled a fresh Monster Big

Suck cup.

Behind the counter, reading a trashy magazine about celebrity UFO abductions was Mrs K, a graying but striking Korean woman in a V-Mart uniform. She had owned the franchise store for ten years and despite the fact she constantly fought with her corporate masters, she loved her store and the kids who treated it as a second home. They were cute for thinking they were the first kids to ever hang in front of a convenience store. Mrs K didn't have the heart to break theirs.

She smiled at Courtney as she came to the counter. There had been no hesitation in letting Courtney have a new Big Suck. She hadn't let her pay for the first one, and there was no way she would charge her for the second.

"Thanks, Mrs K. You're the best," said Courtney.

"How did you do on that history paper?" Mrs K asked.

"Solid. B-Minus," said Courtney. Mrs K raised her hand for a high five. Courtney did not leave her hanging.

Mrs K was always trying to convince the three of them to go to college, but who had time to think that far into the future when none of them could remember to return their rented video tapes to the Blockbuster a town over? (Underwood itself had no video store.)

"Good for you. What are you kids doing for Halloween?"

"Nothing, I think. Audrey wants to dress up and hang out here." Courtney took a careful sip of her Big Suck.

"You should do something other than hang out in my car park," said Mrs K, unimpressed. "I'll give you some expired eggs if you want. You could hit the 7-Eleven near the bypass for me."

"Maybe," said Courtney, non-committal.

"That means 'no'. Jonathan isn't doing anything. You could

go on a date. I made him break up with another Becky," said Mrs K.

"Maybe," said Courtney, some committal.

"That means 'yes,'" said Mrs K, with a knowing smile.

On cue, the door to the back storeroom opened and in slow motion (at least in Courtney's brain) Jonathan K: handsome, tall and chiseled with arms built for performance, entered the store carrying three cases of New Coke. Both his biceps and triceps were bulging and threatening to kinetically exit the confines of his V-Mart uniform. Courtney had checked out an anatomy book from the school library to learn what those muscles were called. She dreamed about seeing his pectorals as well, and other muscles she was too ashamed to find names for. Despite her resistance and resentment at the idea of an all-seeing god, she had still been raised Catholic.

Jonathan locked eyes with her. He smiled and gave her a nod. If Courtney'd been a Big Suck she would have been a puddle on the floor. Without thinking, she took a massive gulp of her new Suck. Instantly her brain snapped, crackled and popped the world back to real time. She grabbed her head in pain. Jonathan kept moving towards the back of the store and she was thankful he hadn't seen her face distorted in ugly brain-freeze pain. She suddenly realized her Suck had gone.

It was sitting on the counter. She had no idea how it had got there. She hadn't noticed Mrs K taking it from her and putting it there before going back to her magazine.

"Jonathan will meet you out front at six tomorrow. Wear something short and tell Audrey to pick up her butts. I see her." Mrs K tapped the CCTV monitor, where it showed the various cameras that covered the store and lot, including the curb.

"You forget my old Coke," said A as C returned to the curb and sat down with the grace of a baby giraffe.

"Sorry, I can't possibly go back in. I have a date tomorrow. My head hurts," she said.

"Halloween!" said A stamping her feet.

"It fell out of my head."

"You suck. It's fine. I get it. I've seen his arms. We should still get costumes."

"I'm in," said B as he held up his arm and tapped an imaginary wrist watch, "You should hustle, it's already 10:45," he said to C.

The three of them stood in unison and walked across the lot towards the intersection. On the way C picked up A's cigarette butt from the ground and tossed it in a bin.

"Give a hoot, don't pollute," said C when A eyeballed her. She didn't want to fuck with Woodsy the Owl either.

At the corner, they waited for the traffic light to turn red and the walk signal to flash green, despite there being zero cars around. Mrs K was always watching, and if they jaywalked, they would hear about it the next day. She was strange about which rules she thought they should follow and which rules were made to be broken.

The V-Mart stood on an intersection where Underwood's imaginatively named Main Street, a six block collection of single-story brick buildings about as post-industrial American small town as you could get, a million others just like in every direction, was bisected by Woodhill Street that ran into the suburbs both north and south. Unsurprisingly, the suburbs of Underwood were both hilly and in the woods.

This was the dead end of town. Main Street ended with little warning a few blocks east in empty overgrown lots and then farmland and then more woods just over the railroad tracks where the interstate abruptly cut it off from the rest of the world. The ramps on and off the highway were at the opposite end of Underwood which had left the businesses down this end of Main Street either closing or already closed. There was almost no foot traffic now. The other end of the street was only marginally better off. Down there was the police station, a liquor store, a bar and the 7-Eleven. They were right by the ramps and the 7-Eleven was the only reason people who didn't live in Underwood got off the highway.

Directly over Woodhill Street from the V-Mart to the west was an overgrown fenced in lot that had been empty since before the three of them had been born. Diagonally across was a Dock's Sporting Goods Store with a large statue of a baseball player with a bat over its shoulder on the roof. South facing the V-Mart was the only restaurant left in town, a Sizzler 'The Original Family Steakhouse' surrounded by an overly-optimistic about the appeal of 'All you can Eat' sized car park with only one car in it at this time of night. This was A's battered blue Ford hatchback. She never parked on the V-Mart lot. Her little engine leaked oil and she didn't want it to stain Mrs K's asphalt. C had questioned her multiple times about why she was fine leaving her cigarette butts anywhere on the V-Mart lot but not oil.

"Screw Sizzler," was A's only answer.

The lights turned red and the crosswalk flashed green but they still didn't move. They were stuck in place by a body-rattling sound of thunder cracking and booming in the cloudless star-filled sky above them.

"Weird," said B looking up.

"A plane?" said C searching the sky.

"You ever wish something would fall out of the sky and crush this shitty town? At least that would be SOMETHING. *War of the Worlds* shit," said A.

B and C both gave her the same look. Worry.

"You're five foot three of gloom tonight," said C.

"I think you're listening to too much Cure," said B as he hugged A. "Night."

She looked him deadpan in the eye.

"It's *The* Cure and I find their unique brand of melodic goth rock to be uplifting. Night."

B chuckled, and A lightly punched him.

"Here, I'm done," said C, handing her Big Suck to B. "My brain still hurts."

B took it, turned and headed west across the street to the empty lot while A and C crossed the other way towards A's car.

Once across the street, B walked past the giant overgrown oak tree on the corner that had broken the chain link fence surrounding the empty lot and cracked the sidewalk, breaking out of its concrete planter box with its escaping roots. He waved as A's car passed him, beeping, and then ducked into the empty lot through the broken fence.

The inside of the lot was a secret playground for teens, hidden from view of the road by trees and the red brick side wall of the Coin-O-Matic laundry. There were stolen shopping carts and the remnants of a rotting half-pipe skate ramp. It was weather beaten with warped boards and rusted nails sticking up all over. B had never seen anyone skating on it. Deep in back, the lot gave way to trees and a creek and the big pipe the three of them had played on when they were younger, before they had rejected physical exertion in principle.

B tripped on *something* in the tall grass halfway to his destination. It was the same *something* he always tripped on but he maintained his balance with his arms wide as he walked quickly towards an old van sitting on blocks tucked near the trees at the back of the lot. On its side was the faded image of the Carpet King, a floating head with beard and crown promising royal carpets at peasant prices. He smirked at all under his gaze. B pulled on the rusted and beat up side door of the van. It made a loud grinding sound and jammed halfway on his first try, so he pulled again, throwing all the weight on his small frame into it, and it unstuck. He jumped in and pulled the door closed behind him with another ear piercing shriek of metal on metal. For weeks he'd been meaning to shoplift some WD-40 from the hardware store to see if he could make his entries and exits quieter, but he kept forgetting.

Inside the van he flicked on a battery powered camping lamp. B wasn't the first kid to use the van as a haven over the years but he was the only one who'd called it home. No one knew when the King went out of business and left his van here, or who the first kid to paste up a Playboy pinup was, but now the walls were covered in them and other photos of bands cut out of magazines. The floor of the van was layered with thick purple shag carpet the King had left behind. B had hung a sheet up to block off the front of the van from the back, 'borrowed' a milk crate from the V-mart for a table and moved in an old wooden chest with a padlock to hide his stuff in: some magazines, some clothes, his questionably sourced and growing collection of fireworks and a small wooden box. The box was the first thing he grabbed after sticking his Walkman headphones on and pressing play on his cassette of *The Ultimate Sin* by Black Sabbath. He fast forwarded past the title track with practiced precision to his favorite song on the album, track two, *Secret Loser.*

B opened the wooden box. Inside was his weed smoking starter kit, papers, various lighters (lost, found and stolen), a small bag of marijuana and half a dozen joints he'd rolled earlier. He took one out and, lying back on a pile of blankets, lit the joint and smoked it. Picking up a set of drumsticks he'd found at school in the music lab, he drummed in time with the song and thought about kissing Annie Munro again.

Outside, thunder boomed again in a stormless sky.

3

Meanwhile, at Vass Corporate Headquarters

It was raining in the city. It fell in torrents against the black marble of the monolithic Vass Enterprises soaring Art Deco skyscraper that stepped back into an ornate spire with tall leadlight windows. When it had topped out shortly after World War II, the local Gazette had called it 'an excessively expensive, miserable, spooky rendition of the Chrysler building.' The Vass family bought the Gazette and shuttered it out of spite, but they'd also secretly loved the description. The tower had been built to make an impression. To show off the family's wealth and power. It was deliberately off-putting. If you looked closely at the intricate details of the mosaics, brass reliefs, gargoyles and statues that decorated the building, you'd probably have come away with the impression that the Vass Empire was built not on the family's excellence in business, but by making dark deals with dark entities. That impression would have been correct.

The boardroom that sat inside the tower's spire was all black marble and real gold trim, lit by dramatic down lights that drew all eyes to a long black stone altar-like table. Sitting alongside it on cold black stone chairs were a dozen old, shriveled, ugly, crooked white men: the heirs to the Vass fortune.

At the head of the table sat the chairman of the Vass board, Maximilian Vass II, a hundred years old and more skeleton than man. His mind was as sharp as the tack he would gladly leave on your chair despite his body's aging betrayal.

"Forecasts for next quarter are grim," he said. His low, gravely voice carried in the space and echoed. The other Vass men grumbled and shared concerned looks.

"Despite our best efforts, we will still only increase profits by 300 per cent," he said with a twisted grin showing off his new teeth, rumored to be carved of ivory. The rumors were true. The men around him laughed on the outside like the joyless jackals they were.

"Yes. Yes. Calm down," Maximilian said, annoyed by their happiness.

"Each of your ample bonus checks is in the mail. Now to new business…"

Maximilian trailed off, distracted. From somewhere else in the building, distant but loud, carried by the flat stone walls of the building came music. It was hard to make out but coming from close by…

"What is that racket?!" said Maximilian in anger.

That racket was *Girls Just Want to Have Fun* by Cyndi Lauper. It blasted out of a Boombox in the Executive Bathroom down the hall as thin fingers with hot pink French tips lowered a metal straw to two neat lines of white powder laid out on a mirror. A petite nose, not all original, snorted twice, hoovering them up. Pupils widened in two stunning, smokey-framed green eyes.

In her grey and pink power suit, Killian Alexandra Vass the First was feeling herself. Her dirty blonde feathered crop did not move as she danced. This was her big night. Well, the prologue to her real big night. That would be Halloween.

Standing behind her were her two meek, virtually identical looking but unrelated assistants. Gina held the Boombox while Tiffany held a shoe-box sized wooden box covered in hot pink occult symbols.

Killian spun to the music with an excited hoot and danced out the door. Gina and Tiffany followed. In the hall, she danced past a long line of oil paintings, a timeline of Vass men. She ignored them, never noticing brothers Giles and Augustus, whose paintings were side-by-side at the start of the row. Giles' painting was giving Augustus' side eye. Even in oil paint, they were still at odds with each other.

At the large set of massive doors leading to the boardroom, Killian slowed and smoothed her suit. *Here we go*, she thought. Years of planning had led to this moment. *Her* moment. Before she could overthink it, she pushed open the doors dramatically and took stage, dancing into the room.

The old men flew into outrage at her intrusion.

"Insolence! What is this?!" yelled Maximilian, standing so fast that Killian heard his bones crack.

Killian ignored him as she danced onto the table using an uncle she didn't know the name of as a footstool. Maximilian slammed his hand down. It boomed through the room loud enough that Killian stopped dancing and threw a look at Gina, who pushed stop on the Boombox.

"What are you doing, you fool girl?" demanded Maximilian.

"Hello Uncles, I'm so glad you're all here in such a convenient mass gathering," said Killian, as sweet as arsenic.

"This is no place for you. Get out!" Maximilian screeched at her.

Killian took her time looking at each of the men. They revealed nothing but disdain for her. To be fair, they showed disdain for most things. But now they had it especially for Killian. They were a collection of so much latent *sexism* that they could have been the dictionary definition of the word.

"Is that so? No. I think I deserve to be here quite a bit more than any of you. I demand a seat on this board, and I'd like that one," she said, pointing at Maximilian's seat.

The Vass men laughed.

Killian laughed back. She was loving this.

"And what makes you think you deserve my seat?" asked Maximilian.

Killian dropped her smile and put up the palm of her hand. Gina pulled out a large leather-bound *grimoire* from the satchel bag around her shoulder and delivered it to Killian. Killian dropped the book down on the table in front of her and knelt down before it.

"I'm glad you asked. It is amazing what you can find in our archives."

Killian flipped the *grimoire* open to a page dense with handwritten text and a woodcut print of The Maw about to red mist Giles and Augustus, who were hanging in the air over the altar with surprised looks on their faces.

"Almost one hundred years ago, my dumb great-great-great-grandfather and his idiot brother had a vision to combine the very best of modern science as they knew it and black magic to rule the world. They failed because of your line. Because of the petty greed and avarice of men like Augustus Alexander Vass whatever the number, your diseased philandering forebearer," she said pointedly at Maximilian.

"How dare you?" he spat at her.

"Oh, I dare, Uncle. I dare more than you ever dreamed. You old withered bitches think money is real power. *Power* is shaping reality. *Power* is twisting the world to fit your vision. What is your vision, Uncle? A chain of convenience stores and a cheap Slurpee knock-off. Your vision is copying your betters. What new flavor are you ripping off this year?" Maximilian raised his withered hand to point to an easel near the far wall where a mock-up ad featured Count Suckula blowing a blue bubble.

"Sour Bubblegum," said Maximilian, chewing each syllable.

Killian rolled her eyes louder than any noise Maximilian could currently make.

"Fool! I will succeed where you have failed. I will return this family to the immortal glory I deserve," Killian scoffed. Maximilian chuckled.

"How? You have no 'power'. Women cannot sit on this board. That's why we buried you in Research and Development. Junior Vice President of wasting your time playing business when you should be at home pumping out a brood of strong male Vass heirs."

"I'm more Vass than you will ever be. It's time for new management," Killian hissed at him through gritted teeth, showing her venom as she closed the book and stood.

Tiffany stepped forward and held the wooden box high as Gina now also stepped up onto the table. Killian slipped her right hand inside the box to grasp something the men could not see. She lifted her hand out. She wore a finger-less mechanical glove covered in occult symbols. It was built from interconnected coiled metal rings and plates over woven mesh.

The rings were thin enough to look fragile but were virtually unbreakable. The plates were larger at the palm and forearm. It looked homemade and dangerous, but was cutting edge black magic tech. Gina strapped a Walkman sized power source with various dial controls and switches to Killian's forearm, plugging it into the glove near the wrist with a thick wire.

The Glove whirred to life with power, its occult symbols glowing.

"What the devil is that?" asked Maximilian.

"I'll show you," said Killian, flicking a switch and turning a dial on the power source. She raised and then closed her gloved hand into a fist.

Her hair blew back music video style…

BOOM!

Thunder ripped through the air as lightning smashed in through the leadlight windows of the spire. Maximilian looked on in terror as the lightning curved around the room and was collected by the glove. It vibrated happily like a kitten who held a tiny mouse on the cusp of death. The glove had somehow *captured* the lightning.

Killian opened her fist with her French tips aimed at Maximilian and the lightning shot out of the glove and blasted him back in his stone chair.

He screamed as the flesh of his whole head melted off his skull like liquid cheese. It was gross. Killian cackled in glee. The other Vass men cowered in fear. The glove was still vibrating and hissing with static. Killian shook it and blew on her nails like they were drying. She felt an almost sexual tingle of pleasure all over her body. She took her time and walked the length of the table. She stopped to push the still smoking corpse of Maximilian Vass out of his seat with her right boot.

She took her throne at the head of the table and looked around at the horrified faces of the remainder of the elderly Vass men. (Two had died of cardiac arrests in the time it had taken her to sit.)

"Hmm, warm. Shall we vote on *my* new business plan?" she asked.

The men around the table nodded so emphatically they almost snapped their ancient necks.

"We only have a day until the centennial," Killian said. "And I plan on making it a day to to remember."

4

A Bricky Fellow

B slept soundly in the Carpet King van, wrapped in the cord of his headphones. The cassette reached the end of the album and stopped with a click.

The violent weather over Underwood was still cloudless, but it was raining heavily. The sound on the roof made B turn over, ensnaring himself even further. Thunder rumbled, and high above the van in the starry sky…

A small rip in space-time appeared like it was no big deal. It started as a single glowing line of light until it cracked out like a car windscreen hit by a flying rock. Its center opened into a jagged wound in reality. From beyond the rip came a nebulously-edged neon blue glowing baseball-sized glass orb. It plummeted in a streak towards the ground, screaming with a human voice. Chasing it came another just like it, except this one was bright red. It screamed, too.

The rip closed faster than it had opened, knitting itself back together and snapping out of existence with a boom of thunder that left the air charged with static.

The blue orb slammed through the roof of the Carpet King

van with a disappointing pop, leaving a circular hole that the red orb fell through seconds later.

Inside the van, the Monster Big Suck cup glowed and swirled as the two orbs now swam within the half-frozen liquid.

"My word, this is odd, brother," said the blue orb with the voice of Augustus Vass.

"What have you done to us? Why am I so cold?" said Giles Vass, the red orb. He tried to press against the plastic of the cup.

"Calm down. We're back! I told you we could get out through that hole," said Augustus.

"Gus, you pillock, we're in some type of tonic. We *are* the tonic!" said Giles, pulsing red.

"Quiet. We're being watched," said Augustus, pulsing blue.

B blinked his red eyes, his face close to the Big Suck cup on his makeshift table.

"He's seen us. Stay still," whispered Giles.

Augustus, always defiant, could not resist himself.

"Hello there, I'm Augustus Alexander Vass the third and this… well, we're? I'm not sure what we are, but we're also my brother Giles. We seem to be sharing this tonic."

B rubbed his eyes. He was pretty sure he was dreaming. Weed before bed always gave him crazy dreams.

"You know in polite society a gentleman introduces himself after being greeted by another gentleman," said Giles.

B flicked on his battery lamp.

Augustus gasped in awe, "What a marvel, brother. This poor person has electricity in his hovel. I've always wanted an outlet for personal use."

B was sure he wasn't dreaming. He bolted backwards and

opened the sliding door with one hard tug, falling onto the wet grass outside. He lay there for a second and laughed.

"I am *so high*," he said, not minding the soft rain falling on him. The inside of the van was stuffy and hot. He looked into the van. It was quiet. He was alone.

When B was little, he'd suffered from night terrors. He'd woken up screaming. His mom had explained to him that sometimes, when you were half-asleep, dream stuff leaked out into our world. That was why he saw the monster at the end of his bed. It had gotten out of his dreams, but it couldn't stay and would be gone by the time he woke all the way up. His dad had told him his mother was full of shit and he needed to be a big boy and get over it. B had stopped telling either parent about his dreams, good or bad, and eventually had stopped screaming in the night as well. Now he shook the damp off his head and climbed back inside the van. He turned to close the door. He froze as the cup spoke again. This was *real*. Someone was talking.

"It's useless, brother. He's an intoxicated vagabond. Hence the tonic at his bedside," said Giles. B turned to face the voices.

"You're a terrible judge of character, Giles. This lad seems rather bricky to me. Just the sort we need. What is your name?" said Augustus.

It was a talking cup. That much was clear to B now. It was just a normal everyday talking cup. That was totally a thing. Also, he was never buying weed from Jessie Bayonne ever again.

"William," he said to the cup. "Mostly I go by Billy. My friends call me B. You lights in the cup are talking, and there are two of you?"

"It's Gus' fault," said Giles.

"Shove off. You only followed me through the hole because I

went first."

"I did not. I would've gone even if you hadn't."

"I was always the brave one. How does it feel to be more scared than your younger, better-looking brother? "

"Get away from me!" whined Giles as his orb pushed against Augustus'.

"No, you get away from me!" Augustus pushed back. The Big Suck liquid tilted as they tried to create distance from each other in the confined space. The cup almost tipped, but B grabbed it and held it up to his face.

"Hey! Yo! If this is real, you both need to start talking, or I'll pour you into the sewer and never do drugs again," he said.

The orbs calmed down.

"It's a long story," said Augustus.

"Let me tell it, brother, or we'll be here all night. You'll add too many embellishments," said Giles. Augustus snorted, and a bubble rose from his orb and popped on the frozen drinks' surface.

"Embellishments are what make a good story, brother," said Augustus.

5

The Pillars of Heaven, Hell &
Underwood High School

Annie Munro walked down the open air hallway past beat up lockers and into the Quad of Underwood High School, a courtyard surrounded by the single-story school with tables for kids to gather and eat lunch.

Annie's blonde hair reflected the golden sun and her cheerleader skirt swished against her long tan legs. Her perfectly white tennis shoes repelled what water from last nights rain was still on the ground. There were a lot of eyes on her, and she knew it. She liked it. From a Boombox nearby, someone was blasting Los Angeles punk icon X's version of *Wild Thing* against the school's policy on playing "music made only by positive role models like Debbie Gibson." Whoever was breaking the rules had no idea they were sound-tracking Annie's life to perfection.

She scanned the Quad nonchalantly. Her large dark blue eyes passed over the Jocks, Populars, Math Squad, Fine Arts Geeks, Drama Queens, Stoners and un-associated others without really looking at any of them. She was deep in *Heathers* territory, she thought to herself. It was her new favorite movie, she'd seen it six times at the movies since it came out earlier in the year, making her Dad drive her the forty-five minutes to the closest multiplex. She couldn't wait till it was out on tape so she could rent it and never return it. While she knew she *looked* like a Heather, on the inside she thought of herself as a Veronica. Today, she wasn't looking for someone who fitted into any of those shallow bullshit social categories. Today she was looking for weirds...

A and C were sitting at a table on the edge of the Quad. A was reading a Christopher Pike book, *The Tachyon Web*, while eating a sandwich. C was drawing in her history textbook with thick POSCA paint pens. She had just turned three crusty founding father douche bags into vampires. Neither noticed Annie until she sat at their table.

"Have you seen William?" she asked, as if this wasn't the start of a seismic social earthquake.

A felt like the entire Quad had turned to watch them. It had.

"What's happening right now?" she asked C in panic.

"William was going to walk me to school and he never showed," said Annie, seemingly nonplussed by their shock.

"It's a complete upheaval of the social order. The pillars are *shaking*," said C.

"Are you sitting with us? Should we stand? Is my face melting?" said A, looking around for answers and getting nothing but shocked looks. This was her greatest fear made flesh: people looking at her.

"I don't care that he flaked. I like that he isn't needy, but I wanted to ask him what you're all going to be wearing for Halloween. I want to try and match thematically but not look like we've *over*-coordinated," explained Annie. "And then I thought, why not just ask you?"

Most of the Quad pretended to lose interest in the conversation, just in case they were next, although the Populars continued to stare. Annie ignored them all.

"I was thinking witches or scary first ladies. I could be Zombie Nancy Reagan, but would people get that?" said Annie.

A screamed with her eyes at C.

"Auds, you could be a perfect Jackie O in her pink suit with a splash of red paint."

C shrugged back at A, and with great caution, A engaged.

"I was thinking witches. Don't call me Auds," she managed to get out as well, fearing verbal retribution that did not come. Instead, Annie picked up the other half of Audrey's sandwich.

"Sure thing, babe. I haven't eaten in a few days. You mind?" said Annie as she sniffed the sandwich and then took a bite before Audrey could answer.

"I'm not wearing green paint. I'll break out. I have a date," blurted out C.

A threw her hands up. What was happening?

"Oh my God, with Jonathan Kang! Shut up. He is so hot. Holy shit! Did you draw this?" said Annie, grabbing Courtney's history textbook and flipping through it.

"I don't… huh… er… what!" said A in desperation.

"Just let it happen. This is too powerful for us to fight," said C.

6

R&D

Killian burst into the Vass Enterprises R&D Lab in her usual fashion with Gina and Tiffany, as always, just a few steps behind her.

The lab was cluttered. Every surface was filled with expensive lab equipment, cutting-edge computers, occult books and strange artifacts. Working away on various projects were half a dozen Vass women, all related either by blood or marriage, arranged more than not, and they were Killian's people. This is where her coup had started ten years earlier. The day after she had found the *grimoire*, now tucked neatly under her arm...

It was called the *Invocatio Dentium* and it was at least a thousand years old. It was filled with tales, myth, folklore, legend, anecdotes, accounts, journeying, scrapbooking and most importantly, methods of ritual related to summoning, bargaining with and pleasing The Great Maw.

Killian gently placed the tome onto a work table where Vlada, a small ancient-looking woman in a lab coat, was using a chunky handheld laser to etch symbols onto an object obscured from Killian's gaze by sparks and light.

"Is it ready?" Killian asked Vlada, her voice unable to mask her excitement.

Vlada flicked off the laser and looked at Killian with a devilish grin. She spoke with a heavily Slavic accent, her voice as rough as her skin.

"Iz ready. Iz perfect," she said.

"It's exact? Just as it appears in the *Invocatio Dentium*? Any deviation could have dire consequences," said Killian, staring at the thing. It was beautiful.

Vlada stroked the cover of the *grimoire* like it was an old lover. Killian and Vlada shared the love of what this book could give them. Power. Real Power.

"Iz juz like book sayz and az describe by stupid man survivor one hundred yearz ago," she said with a playful lilt.

Killian raised an eyebrow. She knew that mischievous tone. Vlada was the widow of one of her great Uncles. She'd been sent to Research & Development fifty years ago to be forgotten. While there, she'd taken a wide-eyed seventeen year old Killian under her wing. According to her now dead father, Killian's obstinate behavior and foul mouth had made her impossible to marry off to even a second or third Vass cousin. Vlada had opened Killian's eyes to the true nature of Vass Enterprises' founding and success: business and black magic, the latter mostly now treated by Vass men as nonsense and veneer so they could play dress ups, get drunk and do vile things to young women. They had tried to bury Vlada in R&D, but unknowingly had put her in the exact position to eventually kill them all.

Vlada had told Killian the truth, how her great, great, great uncles had been real but terrible occultists, dedicated to the rituals and ancient gods found within the *grimoire*. Vlada had guided Killian on where to find it deep in the Vass archives. Vlada had helped her translate the obscured text written to disguise and dead end anyone outside of their circle into plain language. Together they'd devised a plan. Now, not a single male Vass remained alive. They'd had no clue about the uprising that Killian had been fostering. Without a Vass male in this phallic tower of grift and mediocrity, everyone had now been turned to their cause. They were all loyal to Killian and had helped her take over. Now, tonight, they would do what a hundred years of Vass men had not dared to try again.

"What did you do?" asked Killian.

Vlada gestured to Killian's metal gloved hand. Killian had taken to thinking of it as the Power Glove; Nintendo could sue her. Vlada had created it for her. Killian now raised her hand. Vlada flicked the glove on. She turned a small dial Killian hadn't noticed before to five. The glove flowed with energy. Vlada flicked her eyes to the object on her table, and instinctively, Killian knew what her mentor wanted her to do. She moved her hand over Vlada's newest creation, a high tech replica of an ancient triangular Ritual Dagger, a replacement for the long-lost original the Ritual of The Maw demanded. Before she could pick it up, it rose upward and snapped into the glove with a deeply satisfying *kerthump*.

"Magnets!" said Killian, delighted.

"Yez, I add because of great sucking vortex described in original account. Power iz variable," Vlada explained, pointing to a dial on the glove control box. Killian admired Vlada's work on the dagger, running a finger along a blood channel.

"Perfection," said Killian. "Are you sure you won't join us tonight?" she asked.

Vlada shook her head. Killian had already asked her several

times, to her annoyance.

"I am old, thiz magic and glory iz for the young, and besides, it iz premiere of *Alien Nation* the TV show. I will not miz thiz," she said.

"I told you, I'll buy you a VCR."

Vlada grunted and waved her hands in dismissal, turning her back on Killian. The conversation was over. Killian knew Vlada would hear no more talk of her leaving the tower. Killian smiled warmly at her back and then turned to Gina.

"Okay. That's everything, right?" she asked.

Gina opened an overstuffed pink day planner and scanned the page outlining 31 October. "Yes, that's everything. We're all set."

"Great. Let's slip in a pre-ritual nap after yoga but before the shareholders' meeting."

"What, about twenty minutes? A power nap or…"

"You know, I'm dead on my feet after last night, and we are just so far ahead of schedule. Let's make it forty. If I do twenty, by the time I nod off I'll have to get right back up. It'll make me grumpy for the rest of the day. And no one wants that, do they?"

7

Handsome Devils

B slid into the wood-paneled basement rumpus room of his house through the high narrow window, feet first. Once on the ground, he reached back and carefully pulled the Big Suck cup into the room. Like the Carpet King van, B had converted what had once been his childhood play space into a bedroom. His wardrobe was the whole room, black clothes spread everywhere. On the walls were posters of Bruce Lee, Michael Dudikoff as the *American Ninja*, those posters for other games that came with NES cartridges and Playboy pinups that he had self-censored with stickers in case his Mom came down. She never had. Neither of his parents had. His Dad only ever yelled at him from the top of the stairs to come up when they needed to 'talk' to him. 'Talk' was code for yell at. They had let him move down here from his original bedroom upstairs a year ago. It was his way of staying out of his Dad's way when he was home, and it worked for both of them. They had no idea he didn't sleep there and basically only used the house as a place to eat and shower.

"I'm nauseous. Stop swishing us around," said Giles from the

38

Big Suck cup.

"What a thrill!' said Augustus loudly.

"Quiet. My Dad works nights. He's sleeping upstairs," appealed B.

He set the Big Suck cup down on a coffee table in front of the big brown pullout couch. The digital clock on his red plastic TV/VCR combo said it was almost eleven.

"Man, I am so late for school," he said as he shifted a stack of NES games off the couch onto the worn-down brown shag carpet on the floor that, unknown to B, his good friend the Carpet King had laid twenty years earlier.

"Never mind your impending matriculation. We must have our bodies back. We have to find the dagger! " said Giles urgently.

"Yes. If you take us to our Manor, we should be able to retrieve it and sort everything out," said Augustus. B had no idea what they were talking about and his head hurt from lack of sleep. He had spent the entire night with them explaining their situation to him, and the more they talked, the less B had understood. More than once, he'd thought about leaving them in the van and never opening the door again, but his need to help people had gotten the better of him. B dressed tough, but inside, he was a sensitive soul who never said 'no' to anyone.

B took his jacket off and pulled his shirt over his head. He groped around for something that looked vaguely clean. He found his Nine Inch Nails *Pretty Hate Machine* t-shirt. It smelled okay, so he pulled it on.

"Look, I'm still getting my head around this, and I'm cool to help you, but my Dad is a real hard ass and if the school calls him, I'm dead," he explained to the cup people.

"Yes, but we're already dead and on a clock. Tick-tock," said

Augustus.

B picked up the TV remote from the table and turned it on. He pressed play and the VCR whirred to speed.

"Here, watch TV. I'll put the remote next to your cup. I'll be back after class," he said in a rush to stop them from starting to talk again.

"What is 'TV?'" asked Augustus, his orb pushing forward in the cup, clearly already fascinated by the sound and lights.

"I've got to go," B said as he grabbed a pile of textbooks and jammed them into his school bag. He left, quietly stalking up the stairs leading to the rest of the house.

"COME BACK, YOU ROGUE!" yelled Giles.

On the TV, a woman in black heels and a short, tight yellow patterned dress stepped out of a red Ferrari as rock music played.

"Can you believe this, brother? The disrespect!" said Giles, his orb watching the stairs the boy had disappeared up.

"Brother, would you look at this?" said Augustus.

On screen, blue and pink words faded in…

Road House

"We don't have time for this minor sorcery," said Giles.

"One must adapt to our *situation*, brother. I must know of this *Road House*."

"We've already wasted too much time convincing the vagrant to help."

The Big Suck liquid rocked as Augustus' orb pressed close to the plastic.

"Look at that handsome devil," he said.

They watched as Patrick Swayze in high-waisted white pants, a blue polo shirt and perfectly coiffed hair, confronted a man being held by two bouncers.

"They could be right behind us," pleaded Giles.

"If we try to move, we'll spill. Watch this enchanting miniature man."

Swayze turned his back on the man as the bouncers let him go.

The man grabbed a nail file from the table and slashed Swayze on the arm.

Augustus gasped.

"Did you see that, Giles? That villain attacked the handsome man while his back was turned. What will he do?"

The Big Suck shook from both Augustus' excitement and Giles' nerves.

"But brother, *The Teeth!*" exclaimed Giles.

8

Actual Hell or Somewhere Like It

Somewhere else in space and time the lip-less mouth of a creature with human-like teeth chomped open and closed surrounded by off-white fur. It's front facing eyes were bloodshot and its head was bowed to its master.

That master, the being known to the human race as *The Great Maw*, spoke in a guttural boom punctuated by the sound of its own rows of teeth chattering against each other in fury. The language, one of the many it knew, was not capable of being formed by a human mouth with fewer teeth and is translated here for the reader's convenience.

"The supplicants have escaped!" The Great Maw growled to the six nightmare creatures with heads bowed down before it.

THE TEETH.

The creatures were roughly bear-shaped but with stockier shortened rounder limbs that had paws with claws. Each was covered in a different shade of fur. They had various numbers

42

of eyes. Some had horns. Others did not. They had no actual names.

The one with white fur was their de facto leader, *Head Teeth,* with two human eyes. It stood center, front-flanked by the others.

Cyclops Teeth had one eye and dark blue fur.

Spider Teeth was brown and had six small eyes spaced around its head.

The dark purple one had *Gap Teeth* and one of its two eye-holes was stitched shut.

The black one, *Bat Teeth* had bat-like wings instead of paws and no eyes.

The *Horn Teeth* one had bone-white horns, that matched its master's and dried blood-colored red fur with three eyes in a pyramid.

None of them dared looked at The Great Maw.

They waited, eyes down, for instruction. They lived to serve.

"Return the putrid human souls to me," chattered The Great Maw.

Head Teeth roared in affirmation as behind them opened a rip in space-time just large enough for them to pass through.

Head Teeth snapped at the others who one-by-one obeyed, hopping through the rip.

"If one fails, all die," promised The Maw.

Head Teeth chattered its teeth in fear and understanding. It bowed to its master again before it, too, hopped through the rip.

9

What were we up to?

Bran down the empty hall, his Doc Martins thumping hard against the linoleum floor of the hallway. He had never been this late to school. A few periods sure, but not half a day. His side hurt with a stitch; he rarely ran unless being chased. He stopped as he realized he had no idea which class he should be in. He always followed A or C. He stopped and sucked in water from a fountain to cool down and calm his mind. Think, think, think, he thought.

Science!

He turned back the way he had come, now running towards the science block.

Despite B's tardiness, A and C, sitting in the back of class, weren't worried about where he was; they were still stunned from lunch, and they weren't the only ones. The whole school was buzzing with the episode's shocking finale.

The class was rowdy and still taking their seats at rows of work benches. Down near the chalkboard, Mr Luckhurst, a thin man in his forties with a big bushy mustache wiped at his dirty lab coat and then rubbed his temples. His eyes were bloodshot as he took a gulp of coffee from his Erlenmeyer flask. Mr Luckhurst was much loved and talked about at Underwood High. He had recently divorced his wife for a former student, now student teacher, Ms Pollard. The school had only just got over that scandal when she'd left him to be with the head of the English Department, Mr Lawrence. Mr Lawrence drove a convertible and wore a scarf, and most kids thought he was gay. Mostly because of the scarf. The affair and its aftermath had sucked any interest Mr Luckhurst still had left in teaching. These days he often turned up wearing the same clothes as the previous day and smelled of weed and malt liquor. Kids were taking bets on how long till he was fired. Mr Luckhurst coughed loudly to gain their attention.

"Okay, everyone, settle down. Quiet, please. Always so rowdy after lunch, but we are here to learn important heady science stuff and not gossip about schoolyard drama like who sat where and with whom. Although I heard Annie Munro sat with some unpopular kids today. Is that *true?*"

C raised her hand. Mr Luckhurst pointed at her but said nothing.

"That was us," said C.

A climbed onto her stool to address the class. For just a moment Mr Luckhurst thought she was going to 'Captain, my captain' him.

A cleared her throat.

"It shook us to our very core," she said. "We would ask you to respect our privacy in our time of…"

C pulled A down from the stool.

"Don't make it worse," said C.

Mr Luckhurst was saddened and perplexed. The class took

this as an invitation to start talking again.

"Yeah, I can see how that would be challenging. What's with that? You know what, never mind. We are here to… QUIET!" he yelled. The murmurs subsided.

"We are here to learn about the stuff of life, life cycles and whatnot, biology. Er, does anyone remember where we're up to?" he asked.

C raised her hand again. Mr Luckhurst pointed at her once more.

"Ripley had just found Newt."

Mr Luckhurst dragged over the cart with the TV and VCR on it to the center of the room. He pulled a home-recorded VHS copy of *Aliens* out of his lab coat pocket and jammed it into the player. He pressed play, then started to rewind.

"Are you sure?" Mr Luckhurst asked. "I thought we'd already gotten to the facehugger scene." He made a chestburster gesture with his hand while making the noises and everything.

The door to the lab flew open as B entered, sweating. Mr Luckhurst stopped his chestburster hand mid-fight with himself. The whole class looked at B.

"Sorry. What are we up to?" B said between ragged breaths.

"Apparently Ripley just found Newt," said Mr Luckhurst.

"I thought we'd finished *Aliens*," B said earnestly.

The class booed and threw paper at him. Someone even tossed a Bunsen Burner, but it missed wide and hit the floor with a clang.

"Oh, leave him alone," Mr Luckhurst said. "I know we all enjoy the ruse of where we are up to, but *John Carpenter's The Thing* isn't on TV till next week, and I only own one tape, so it's *Aliens* until then. Go take your seat." Mr Luckhurst rewound the tape as the class settled down. Eventually he found the scene he was looking for.

"Okay. Enjoy the movie,' he said. "Make sure you're learning. Look out for, you know, any *biology*. I'm going to be in my office doing other science. Don't inhale any smoke you see and yell out if anyone spots the VP headed this way."

Mr Luckhurst exited to his storeroom, shoulders hunched.

"I had the longest, craziest night," said B as he sat with A and C, drumming his hands on the bench.

A and C were not impressed. C ignored him entirely. She flicked open her science textbook and started drawing over an image of Ben Franklin.

"Where have you been? *Annie* sat with us," said A. B's face lit up with a goofy smile and he paused mid drum.

"Really, that's awesome," he said as he flicked on the table gas outlet and took a whiff of the good stuff.

A flicked the tap off in annoyance.

"What? No? It was *terrifying*. The whole school is in an uproar. People *know* who we are," said A.

"It was a total freak show," said C, not looking up from her art.

"I told you she's really into me," said B.

A grabbed his arm and looked him straight in the eyes.

"We're going costume shopping at four. She wants to be witches. Witchii? What is the plural of witches? What have you done? I'm too weird to be a cool," said A.

B checked his non-existent wristwatch.

"I don't think I can make that."

A squeezed B's arm hard until she saw him wince in pain.

"*Do not* leave me alone with her. I already used *all* my expressions. She'll find me out," she pleaded.

"Where were you all morning?" asked C in a more reasonable

tone.

"You are never going to believe me," said B.

The bell rang. A, B and C exited the science lab into the packed hallway. C tried to ignore the many eyes on them. She could feel the gossip like it was a living breathing thing trying to suffocate them, like that stupid *Blob* movie.

"You don't believe me?" B asked, knowing the answer. "I can't believe you don't believe me." B had told them everything he could remember about the last thirteen hours of his life and they had stared at him blankly, except for A's almost reflexive eye rolling.

"No, I don't. You're a bad liar," said A.

"A bad liar, how?" asked B.

"For starters, you tell lies badly," stated A.

"Courtney?" said B, appealing to her.

C was caught off guard. B only ever called her Courtney when he was very serious. She was dubious about his story but wanted to give him another chance to explain. She wasn't sure she had caught all the details. She'd been deep into making Ben Franklin the Bride of Frankenstein.

"You're saying the souls of two old dudes escaped hell or something?" she said, half recounting, half asking.

"The way they described it, it was as an alternate dimension that is the basis of all Judaeo-Christian hell myths, but I'm not a hundred per cent on that," B answered.

"Sure, *that's* what you're unclear on," said A.

A freshman passing the other way got too close. A bared her teeth and hissed like a cat, scaring him off and giving him a story he'd recount with great gusto to an enraptured audience in the freshman boys' bathroom ten minutes into the future.

By then, his retelling included A pulling a knife on him.

C stopped in front of her locker. The inside of the door was a shrine of magazine cutouts: Stevie Nicks, Iggy Pop, David Bowie and David Niven. A and B had never asked C about the last one, to her annoyance.

"So these guys ended up in 'hell,' enslaved to a pissed-off demon god thing?" asked C as she dumped her books inside.

"What about Janice?" said B to A, momentarily ignoring C.

"What's a Janice?" said A as she handed her textbooks to C.

"Janice was your imaginary friend who lived in your credenza," said B as he passed his textbooks to C as well. C put them all in her locker. They shared it. B didn't know where his actual locker was, and A was never going near hers again after what she called the 'talking yogurt incident'.

A crossed her arms defensively.

"I do not remember that at all. I didn't have imaginary friends. I was too lonely."

"And now the two old dudes?" asked C, wanting to piece everything together.

"Augustus and Giles," said B.

"Right, Augustus and Giles, who are stuck in a V-Mart Big Suck that's somehow still frozen?" asked C.

"Yeah. I don't know how. They want me to take them to their manor to retrieve a magical dagger so they can finish a ritual and get their bodies back," he said.

"Right, yeah, a dagger," C said, deciding whose side she was landing on. "So, how high were you?

"I was toasted, but it happened, I swear," said B, disappointed.

"I believe you," said C in a tone so dry that B missed her sarcasm.

"Thank you," he said to her. "How don't you remember your

imaginary friend?" B stood in front of A, his hand on her shoulders. "Rich sold the credenza at a yard sale. When you found out, you convinced me to break into the new owner's house so you could say goodbye. I believed you. I helped you commit a B&E. That's a felony. That's straight time. That's *Eddie Bunker* time."

"Is this because I said nothing ever happens here?" A asked. "I appreciate the effort, but you could have just set the bubblegum factory on fire again."

Again, thought C. Wait, what? She couldn't connect her thoughts fast enough. B's frustration rushed out of him.

"This is *real*! It's happening. They have to do it tonight, or they have to wait another hundred years. I can't have them live with me that long," he yelled.

"Because *Halloween*?" said A.

B slumped against the locker. He looked defeated.

"Yeah. Halloween, I think. I haven't slept and they both talk a lot. You really don't believe me?"

"I don't want to verbally dagger you in the heart, but maybe Mr T was right… 'Don't do drugs,'" said A.

"Okay. Wow. Dude. I'll just have to show you. Meet me this afternoon at the V-Mart," B said as he stormed away down the hall.

"We have to get costumes!" A yelled after him.

"Janice?" asked C. "I don't get that reference."

"I thought it was a pretty name. I was four. I was an idiot."

"Are you punishing him for Annie?"

A closed C's locker aggressively.

"No. *Yes.* It's been the three of us forever. Can you her sitting on the curb out front of the V-Mart every night? It's boring. She's probably allergic to boring," said A.

"And what about Jonathan?" asked C.

"He has to be there. He works there," said A, rubbing her face and sighing. "Hey, you want to skip Math and English?

C shrugged yes, and wordlessly they started down the hall towards the exit.

"I don't like being looked at," A said. "It makes me feel *seen*."

10

Mass

B slid through the narrow window and back into the basement. On the TV there was static, and on the coffee table the Big Suck cup was lying on its side. Its frozen sludge was leaking around the TV remote and dripping off the table onto the brown carpet.

B ran over in panic. "Dudes? Old Dudes?"

"See, brother. I told you the lad would return," said Augustus weakly.

Their orbs were half-submerged in the cup and they were melting. The glass orbs that were contained them had magically assimilated with the sludge at its edges while the rest of the orbs held their form. They had started to become part of the drink.

B picked up the cup and they almost spilled out.

"Stop! Unhand us, you cretin!" said Giles.

B put the cup back down on its side with care.

"What happened?" he asked.

"A simple mishap," said Augustus cheerfully.

"A mishap? *You* tipped us over!" scoffed Giles.

"I was merely trying to re-conjure the fascinating, handsome man. Tell me, young William, are all men of this era so strong and yet vulnerable like this 'Dalton?'" asked Augustus.

It took B a second to clock what Augustus was talking about. Who was 'Dalton'? Ah, the dude Swayze played in *Road House* was named Dalton. B had no strong opinions on Dalton. He liked *Road House* okay. The throat rip and monster truck running over the car yard scene ruled. Swayze kicked ass. The doctor lady was hot. The music was lame. He dug that John Doe from the seminal Los Angeles punk band X was in it, even if he got his ass kicked and didn't play music. He realized that none of this was entirely relevant to his current situation.

"Forget the tiny dandy and his womanly affectations. We must re-acquire mass," said Giles.

"I must know. Is his philosophy popular among men of your time? To be nice until it is no longer time not to be nice?" Augustus asked, not be dissuaded.

"It's a popular movie. I had to wait a couple of days for the tape to come back into the store," answered B.

"A 'movie', you say and what is that?" asked Augustus.

The conversation was not going the way B had thought it would on the long walk over from the school on the other side of town. He had not run this time. On his way back, he had started to hope he'd been making everything up and that when he got home there would be nothing on his coffee table but un-returned videotapes and a melted - and silent - Big Suck.

"Ah, man. A movie is like a story… like a play but not boring and it's on film," he said.

The cup shook with laughter.

"It's a foolish entertainment for the masses. Your new hero, Dalton, is nought but a lowly thespian!" said Giles.

"Hold your tongue!" Augustus barked. "Don't you see we're stuck here in the future? We must work together. How is it that I'm having to be the rational one?" he asked.

"I'm sorry, brother. I'm not handling this very well. I'm hysterical. Almost womanly so. You are right. We should be men about it."

"Thank you, brother. I don't know why you don't follow my lead. I'm almost always right. As Dalton says. 'My way or the highway.'"

B had to get this all sorted and get rid of these guys so he could meet A, C and Annie.

Annie would believe him, wouldn't she? B had no idea if she was into science fiction. *Non*-fiction science fiction. Was that even a thing?

"You said something about mass?" B said, trying to get them and himself to focus.

"I did. We are losing size at an alarming rate. I can feel my edges dripping away. It's unpleasant," said Giles.

"I can get you a refill, but I'm going to have to slide you back into the cup."

"Fine, but be gentle," said Giles.

"Pain do not hurt, brother," Augustus snickered.

B used his hand to keep them in the cup as he lifted it upright.

"That's not even proper English," said Giles, slurring as they slid back into the depths of sludgy safety.

11

"Thanks for Shopping V-Mart"

Jonathan handed a customer their change and thanked them for shopping at V-Mart. He tracked the customer across the multi-view security monitor, watching until they drove off the lot. He checked the store to make sure he was alone and then picked up the remote for the store's four ceiling-mounted TVs. His Mom insisted they were only to play tapes for V-Mart promotions during the day, just in case someone from Vass Enterprises Franchise Relations came by. She didn't care what was on after five. Right now on the TV, Count Suckula was standing in a cemetery set that Ed Wood would have called cheap and tacky, while he offered two Monster Sized Big Sucks for the amazing price of just one.

"Suck with, or on, your friends…" said Count Suckula. He laughed spookily, but not quite in the right key.

Jonathan knew he was taking a risk, but he flicked through a couple of channels to find MTV anyway. The video for *She Drives Me Crazy* by Fine Young Cannibals was just finishing. Jonathan was confused by their name. Who ate human flesh and was still an upstanding citizen? It just didn't make any sense.

The next video started.

"Yes!" said Jonathan to the empty store. It was *The Look* by Roxette. Jonathan loved Roxette. They were so cool with their blond hair and Swedish good looks. He wondered if Courtney liked Roxette. He'd noticed she always wore band T-shirts, which was cool. It was one of many things he liked about her. He'd made a mental list.

1. She was tall.
2. She smiled at him every time she came into the store.

That was the whole list.

Now he added:
3. She always wore band T-shirts.

They'd only spoken a couple of times, but he'd always been too shy to move past 'hello'. He'd thought about asking her out when they were at school together. She'd been a sophomore when he was a senior. Jonathan had graduated two years before and was now at community college studying economics. He didn't like it. He wanted to drop out and open a gym. His hero was Arnold Schwarzenegger. He'd rented *Pumping Iron* a dozen times from the video store. His Mom said he needed to graduate first. He wasn't going to argue with her. She had worked her butt off waitressing full time, learning English, studying business at night school and raising him as a single Mom before she'd gotten enough money together to buy the Underwood V-Mart franchise. Jonathan was proud of her. He didn't mind that she tried to run his life. It meant he could focus on his personal goal of getting bigger and stronger in the gym. He did wish she would stop making him break up with girls. He'd liked Becky Martin a lot. Then again, he liked the idea of Courtney Vazquez more.

Once the coast was one hundred per cent clear, Jonathan spun the sunglasses carousel and grabbed a pair of knock-off V-Mart 'Vass-Bans'. He put them on and picked up his mop. Right as the chorus hit, he slid *Risky Business* style into the store's middle aisle. He hadn't seen *Risky Business*, but everyone knew the dance scene. Using the mop as his microphone, he sang along loudly to the song as he cleaned. He had moves, and he knew it. As he scrubbed the linoleum, his hips were doing most of the work.

Jonathan danced oblivious past the front windows of the store where A and C were staring at him with their mouths agape. The sound of the music was dulled by the double glazing of the windows.

"This is just…" A trailed off. She legitimately felt like she should not be seeing this. This should be just for C. Still, she was not going to look away. She had needs, too. Confused as they sometimes were.

"No talking," said C.

"But, butt…"

"Quiet butts. Let him clean. It's important he cleans," said C as she pretended to smoke a cigarette.

A lit a real one and forced herself to turn away. She sat on the curb and instantly felt better.

"Hips," drooled C, standing above her.

"Sit down. Today has been…"

"Too much," said C as she peeled herself away from the vision of Jonathan K's ass and sat next to A.

They had spent the afternoon dreading four o'clock and their costume date with Annie. C had argued for bailing, but A worried that it could make things worse.

"What if Annie decides to make another scene, but this time she yells at us?" asked A. It had spiraled from there. A had told C she was prepared to leave town forever, but didn't think she would survive long living life on the rails as she imagined they would be forced to do if they missed their date. Jumping trains. Sleeping under overpasses. Making soup from old belts. Fighting trolls. It wasn't fair. C had her size on her side. A was a morsel, snack-sized, ready to be chewed up and spat out by the first depraved madman carrying a bindle who seemingly befriended them by offering leftover chili and a warm fire to cool their heels by. Sure, Old Ben seemed nice and said the right words. Then you were human steak. A didn't really like red meat and even more so didn't want to *be* it.

C had agreed that yes, life on the road like this would not be ideal.

Needless to say, the chat had not been their most productive. Now it was almost four and they had still not skipped town. They really should have been walking up Main Street to meet Annie, but they both needed a second to recover from those biceps, triceps, other ceps and, undeniably, his hips. The word 'glutes' floated through C's head. She saw Jonathan posed in one of her anatomical books and blushed.

Unseen behind them in the store, Jonathan kept dancing as he wiped the glass fronts of the row of fridges in time to the music. Just as he wiped the New Coke fridge, he swore he saw something move right at the back, like a flash of white or something, maybe. He stopped wiping and pressed his face closer to the fridge. The glass fogged, making it harder to see in. The sound of crashing glass coming from the storeroom behind the fridges made him jump back. Was someone in here? Had they seen him dancing? He would have been so embarrassed if they had.

He walked slowly to the storeroom door on the back wall of the store. He turned the knob and pushed the door open an inch. He peered inside. A crack of daylight sliced through the dark of the room to reveal a broken crate of milk bottles. Jonathan pushed the door some more and peered in further.

There was a hole in the roof. It created a shaft of light that cast a monstrous shadow on the storeroom wall. His mother was going to be so mad with him. Why did bad things only happen when *he* was in charge? In the store, *The Look* ended. Then Jonathan saw *it*. He had no idea what *it* was, but he saw *it*.

The source of the shadow was a tiny monster, barely a foot tall.

Head Teeth growled at him from on top of a stack of Miller Lite cartons. It took a running leap. Jonathan reeled back from the thing now flying towards his face, swatting at it and missing. He fell to the floor of the storeroom as more tiny monsters emerged from behind the cartons to join the attack, chattering their teeth in a ferocious war cry. Despite their size, they were stronger than you'd think. Their breath was hot as they snapped their teeth at Jonathan's face and neck and he struggled to get them off.

On the TVs in the store, the sound of the video for *Cult of Personality* by MC5 drowned out his screams. Outside, A finished her cigarette. She was about to flick it when she saw the look C was giving her. She stopped herself, stood and put it in the trash bin near the front door.

"We should go meet Annie," said C.

"Fine," said A.

They walked away just in time to not see Jonathan stumble out of the storeroom as he attempted to escape The Teeth leaping from shelf to shelf as they chased after him.

12

Slow Harry's Halloween Emporium

Underwood was so off-brand that it didn't even have a Spirit Halloween. Instead it had a Slow Harry's, which wasn't even a real costume shop. It had opened in the closed-down other laundry halfway down Main Street. Whoever had had the bright idea to open a second laundry in town was an idiot, and it had gone out of business within a few months of opening and then sat empty for years. While some people in town had seen it as yet another reminder of recession on Main Street, Slow Harry, whoever the hell he was, saw an opportunity to fill a gap in the market for the upcoming spooky season. His emporium had held its grand opening only the week before to a shrug from Underwood adults and fascination by its teens and preteens alike. Slow Harry hadn't even bothered to move out the washers and dryers. Instead, he had filled them with plastic skeleton parts and red food dye.

They swished back and forth on rinse as Annie rushed past them towards the overflowing randomly laid out racks of women's costumes. A and C followed her at a more reasonable pace. They had been there thirty seconds.

Annie was amazed by everything.

A wanted to die.

C was still thinking about Jonathan's hips.

Annie pulled out matching witch costumes and held them up to A. Her eyes were so wide you could see the front of her brain.

"We could totally shock in these if you wear the pink and I wear the black," Annie squealed.

"If you Ally Sheedy *Breakfast Club* me, I will chew your face off," said A, folding her arms unimpressed. A hated John Hughes and his cloying bullshit about how teens were all the same inside. She knew he was wrong. At thirteen, she had written him a four page letter to tell him that. He'd sent back a signed photo. B had burnt it for her.

"I would never Ally Sheedy you. Your gloom is a statement," Annie said, looking affronted .

"Like a cat once its owner dies. The whole thing. All the soft bits," A said, feeling like she needed to push home her point.

"You are wicked. I love your whole grrr. Try on the black. Pleeeeese. You will slay," said Annie.

A had to admit to herself that the dress was cute, if a little too revealing for her usual style, but it was Halloween, and she was the one who wanted to make it a thing. The idea of slaying also appealed, but for a more literal interpretation than Annie knew. A snatched the black dress out of Annie's hands and took it to the change room with an exaggerated sigh. There was no way she was going to let Annie know she liked it.

"Why did I get what I wanted and still feel screwed?" A muttered as she walked away.

C waited patiently until A was out of earshot and turned to

Annie.

"I need your help. Make me a hot like you. I have a date with Jonathan Kang tonight. I must know your ways," she begged Annie.

Annie put her hand to her heart.

"Oh, babe," she said. "After I finish with you, Jonathan K is going to just *die*."

13

Dokka-beccy?

The V-Mart's doors dinged open as Mrs K rummaged through her vast handbag for something she had already forgotten she was looking for in her brisk walk across the lot.

"Jonathan, head office called and said someone is coming by tonight for some reason. I wasn't listening, but I'm going to yell at them about the New Coke situation."

Her ears pricked up, hearing *Everybody Wants to Rule the World* by Tears for Fears on the TVs instead of the V-Mart promo tape. She lifted her head to admonish Jonathan, but stopped dead when she saw the state of the store. It was trashed. The floor was covered in ripped packaging, food and broken glass. The fridge doors were swinging open. The hot dog machine was making wet grinding noises as if the dogs were screaming for help.

Amid the chaos, The Teeth were having the time of their lives. Gap Teeth chewed a Baby Ruth still in its packet, Horn Teeth was flipping through the October issue of Playboy with Pamela Anderson on the cover, Spider Teeth had built a web of red vines and strange white goo between two of the TVs and was napping. Closest to Mrs K, Bat Teeth perched like a tiny gargoyle on a display stand for *Batman: The Movie* cereal shaped like the Gotham City skyline.

Bat Teeth saw Mrs K and took off in a wide arc, flapping its wings at full stretch. It gained height, lining her up. Then folded its wings back and swooped at her, chattering its teeth.

Mrs K watched it the whole way then casually backhanded it into a shelf of Doritos as soon as it was near enough. It rubbed its head with its bat wings.

"What the fuck is this?" she swore in Korean.

"Mom?" said Jonathan from behind the counter. Mrs K walked around to find Head Teeth and Cyclops Teeth threatening Jonathan with plastic sporks as he sat on the floor holding them off with what was left of his mop. The handle was chewed down to less than half its original length. Head Teeth turned, chomped his teeth and growled. Mrs K flicked it hard on the nose.

"No," she said. Head Teeth blinked and took a step back. It rubbed its nose then shook its head in anger and crouched down like a cat that was about to pounce. Mrs K pointed her finger at it firmly.

"*Aniyo*," she said. 'No' in Korean.

Head Teeth hesitated like it might have understood her and then snapped its teeth at her finger.

"I said *aniyo*," she said forcefully.

Cyclops Teeth, who had turned to see what was happening, chattered at Head Teeth, goading it to attack. Head Teeth chattered back a sharp command and Cyclops Teeth backed off.

Mrs K picked them both up by their ears. They wailed in

pain. Head Teeth tried to bite her, but Mrs K kept them at a safe distance.

"Oh, shoosh. Enough!. It doesn't hurt," she said in Korean. The Teeth stopped complaining but kept squirming. Jonathan, his face cut and bleeding, looked on in amazement. He'd been fighting these monsters off for an hour and it'd only taken seconds for his Mom to stop them in their tracks.

"That's better." Mrs K turned to her son. "Jonathan, what have you let these *dokkaebi* do to our store?" Jonathan stood up and rubbed his face. He was very worried about his face. He checked it in the sunglasses carousel mirror.

"Dokka-beccy?" he asked, looking like he'd been attacked by angry cats.

Mrs K searched her mind for the English words, "Ah... *dokkaebi*... goblins. Tiny demons," she said. She wasn't one hundred per cent sure that that was what they were, but it was close enough. *Dokkaebi* were mischievous spirits that her father had warned were always watching her when she was a child. She'd grown up fearing them but also wanting to have one as a friend who could grant her wishes. Right now, they were a pain in her ass that would have to be dealt with as soon as head office had left.

"Grab the other ones," she instructed. "We'll lock them in the office."

Jonathan was confused. "Goblins? Like *The Muppets?*"

Mrs K gave him a look that he knew meant forget about it and just do what he'd been told.

"Halloween is always a good time for *dokkaebi* to cause trouble. Never mind them. We have to tidy the store before head office gets here," she said as she walked towards her office behind the counter. "Why they are coming tonight, I do not know," she continued as she pushed open the door with her hips and disappeared from Jonathan's sight.

Jonathan looked at the other Teeth. They'd heard the commotion and had gathered on the top shelf of the bread stand to watch what was happening.

"You know we didn't even get an invite to the shareholders' meeting. Like my stock is printed on toilet paper!" Mrs K yelled out as he stared at the tiny monsters. He was unsure about getting any closer, let alone picking one up. His fingers were nearly as important as his face.

"Oh, and you have a date with Courtney tonight, so hurry up!" Mrs K said, poking her head through the office doorway.

Jonathan smiled, showing his own teeth. Unfortunately for Jonathan, The Teeth took this as a threat and jumped at him.

14

The Shareholder Meeting

In the palace-like auditorium of the Vass Enterprises building a screen showed a black and white close-up of Killian's power-gloved hand running over long grass. A voiceover that sounded a lot like Angelica Huston accompanied the imagery.

"Killian Vass offers a new vision of the future for Vass Enterprises… and the world."

Killian sat in the back row of the theater with her bare feet up on the seat in front of her, mouthing along to the words.

"A future where ancient black magic and modern technology work hand-in-hand to not just deliver profits, but to manifest a better world."

On screen, Killian stroked the mane of a horse. Then she stood high and windswept atop a dramatic outcrop of rock as the camera circled her. Below her, a bunch of horses ran wild and free through a majestic canyon.

Gina walked down the aisle and knelt next to Killian.

"We should send Ridley a hamper or something. He really knocked this out of the park," said Killian. She had loved his campaign for New Coke with Max Headroom, and the fruit computer thing had been okay, even if it was a little lefty. This film had been her idea. Who wanted another boring speech with slides and handouts when you could make something people would *feel* as well as be informed by?

Tiffany, sitting next to her, opened a leather notebook in her lap and scribbled down a reminder with a pen that had a light on it.

"It's time. The ritual team is ready," whispered Gina. Killian raised her finger to her mouth to silence her.

"One second, this bit is important," said Killian.

"Vass Enterprises is thrilled to announce that at the center of Killian's vision is a new partnership: a partnership that spans *dimensions*," said maybe Angelica Huston.

Gina turned to go, but stopped herself. Now was as good a time as ever. She gave herself an unspoken, "You can do this," and turned back to Killian.

"Boss, I have some concerns about my employment agreement," she said as boldly as she dared. Killian didn't look at her. Her eyes were full of her own cinematic vision.

"Hmm. Have you spoken to HR?"

Gina's heart sank, but she had started now, so she pushed on.

"I love working for you, but I'm not sure being a sacrificial virgin is the best thing for my career," she said as confidently as she could muster.

Tiffany closed her notebook, stood up and walked away. She wanted no part of this conversation. She'd lost her own virginity to one of the greasy Vass mail room miscreants as soon as she'd first heard of Killian's 'plan.' It was a small price to pay. Sure, she'd lost some shine in Killian's eyes, but she was also free and clear of a dagger to the heart and promises about an afterlife she wasn't sure even existed.

Killian now looked at Gina as if she had just killed Killian's favorite cat. Killian thought cats were too needy, but she loved how they brought you dead things as a treat. She loved it so much she had the R&D team strip the flesh of the "treats" with acid so she could display their bones on her mantle.

"I…" Gina tried to pull the emergency brake on the conversation, but it was too late. Killian wasn't just angry, she was also disappointed.

"Gina, Gina, Gina. Do you know how many young people would die, literally, to be in your position at your age?" Killian was all ice. Gina lowered her eyes.

"I know. It's just that… I'm…"

This time Killian raised her voice to a level the whole theater could hear. The audience did not move.

"When I was your age… the hours I worked… the rituals I took part in. I'd have *killed* to be where you are. I *did* kill to get where you are. I killed a lot of people, but that's not the point. It would help me if you thought about how much exposure this is going to get you in other dimensions. People will know your name, and I have our best lawyers and sorcerers ready to work on getting your soul back as soon as the partnership is complete."

Gina was firmly back in her place. "Okay. You're right. I'm sorry," she said meekly. She *was* sorry she brought it up. She *was* willing to die for Killian. At least that was the lie she told herself.

"It's okay. I just want you to appreciate the opportunity I've given you," said Killian, her rage passing like a summer storm leaving rainbows with edges so sharp they could cut you. She turned back to the screen.

"I do appreciate it. Thank you," said Gina.

Gina heard her mother's voice in her head telling her she should have gone to beauty school so she had a trade to fall back on.

"Oh, I missed the best part. Can we run it again?" Killian asked.

Gina checked the pink luminescent dial of her watch and shook her head. "There's no time left."

Killian's nap had run ninety minutes too long and had put everything behind, but Gina would never have said that even before her most immediate *faux pas*.

Killian pushed herself out of her chair like a moody teen and walked down the center aisle. Gina followed her, trying not to look at the hundreds of Vass Shareholder corpses (now all *former* shareholders), who comprised the audience. Most of their faces were melted like candle wax. Those who still had features looked shocked to be dead.

15

Substitutionary Locomotion & Transmogrification

The door of the V-Mart dinged open and B rushed in holding the cup containing Augustus and Giles.

"Yo, Mrs K?" he called out.

No one answered. The now pristine store was empty. B headed straight for the hulking Big Suck machine on the back wall of the store near the fridges, the burrito microwave and the hot dog machine. He placed the cup on the tray beneath the dispensers too quickly, forcing the orbs of Giles and Augustus to slosh around in a miniature ice-flecked tsunami.

"Careful. Thoughtless wretch!" shouted Giles.

B stared at the machine. A problem had occurred to him.

"Ah… what flavor?" he asked.

"Oh. Perhaps Pluto Water, if they have it? But nothing with opium in it. It blocks me all up," said Augustus excitedly.

B broke the news. "They have Apple Raspberry, Cola, Cherry and Sour Bubblegum - ooh, that's new."

"Let me think," said Augustus.

"Gus?" said Giles impatiently.

"I think *I* should choose brother. You'll no doubt pick something fruity."

"No, brother, I have an idea. Do you remember that butter-and-egg fly Irish woman that prattled on about that Substitutionary Locomotion Invocation?"

Augustus' orb glowed brightly.

"I do, Giles. She was quite a sport, I remember. Yes, if our friend here were to pour us into the bulk of the tonic mass…"

"Yes, it might just work. See what happens when you agree with me?."

B was so lost. "So… Cola or…?"

"We need you to pour us into the body of this tonic machine and then open the tap above our current receptacle when we say so," said Giles, like it should have been as plain as day.

"Alright," said B, picking up the cup, more carefully this time. He headed to the storeroom door that he knew led to the back of the Big Suck machine.

He just missed Jonathan coming out of the office. Jonathan was wearing pressed black pants, a tight white collared short-sleeve shirt and a skinny black tie. He had a band-aid on his face over the largest scratch. He hoped Courtney wouldn't notice the others.

His mother was still in the office trying to get answers from The Teeth, but she paused to see him off on his date.

"Ah, no. Quiet," she said. The Teeth piped down. She joined Jonathan in the store, closing the office door. She gave him a little push.

"Go. Have a nice time. Make a move."

"Mom." Jonathan blushed. This was the one part of his life he wished she would stay out of. He knew he had no chance of that happening.

"Go. Make a move. Now!"

Jonathan left as the video for *Spellbound* by Siouxsie & the Banshees started to play.

He could still hear the song as he stepped onto the lot. The sun was low, casting strong hard shadows across the car park. He shielded his eyes and saw Courtney with Audrey and Annie Munro. He didn't know they knew each other. They were walking, back lit in slow motion, only for him.

Courtney looked stunning. They all did, but he only saw her. She was poured into a Victorian-era red dress. She'd added glam rock embellishments to it, pinned on a swatch of sequins, band pins and sewn on a patch near her heart that said "Die Hot." She'd cut the bottom of the dress, angled to look like it was torn. You could see her long legs and combat boots. She was a glam rock time traveling *queen*.

A and Annie had gone bad and good witches like Annie had wanted, black and pink, respectively. A had framed her eyes with thick black eyeliner and powdered her face even paler than its natural pallor. Her black hair, at Annie's insistence, was spiraled up and hairsprayed to death. She was wearing Converse All Stars for comfort (she had violently refused heels). Blood red lipstick finished the job. She was the bad witch.

Annie was every bit her opposite. Her blonde hair was big and teased, her shoulders were padded, her dress was short and layered like a tutu. Her long tanned legs and pointed pink heels gave her even more height over A. She was the good witch to a T.

They arrived at the front of the store. In Jonathan's brain, time returned to normal.

Annie pulled A back a few steps to give C and J space.

"Hey," said C, trying to sound cool. It worked.

"Hi," said Jonathan, trying not to sound totally overwhelmed by her beauty. It did not work.

"What happened to your face?" she asked, reaching up and almost touching him but pulling back when she caught what she was doing. She couldn't just touch his *face*. That was not a jawline you could simply invite yourself to enjoy. His cheeks were so sharp they would probably cut her fingers. His chin was like art, meant to be looked at and discussed in Parisian salons. The dress had put her in a very peculiar head space.

"Oh, cats," said Jonathan as a cover. "Mean cats."

Jonathan gestured for them to walk. C looked around for the mean cats.

"Really? Where are they now?" she asked. Jonathan regretted his lie but was committed now. He tried to dig up.

"Gone back to where… they came from. To where cats go…" he said. C decided to change the subject. She didn't care. She gestured to a red Nissan 200SX parked in front of the store.

"That's yours?"

"Yeah."

"Cool."

C went to the passenger door and waited. Jonathan stood clueless for a second before coming around to open the door for her. She struggled to get in without showing him more than she wanted to, at least for now. She was open as to how many bases he might get to later. He helped her in with his eyes averted and then jogged around to the driver's side and got in. She smiled at him. He smiled back. He didn't start the car. This was not going well. C realized she had no idea if they had anything in common except the low hum of mutual lust.

"Should we go?" C prompted him.

He took a big breath. "Yeah. Okay."

He opened his door to get out.

"What…?" said C.

Sitting on the curb, watching smugly, A took a drag of her cigarette. Annie was standing so she wouldn't ruin her dress. A didn't care.

"…is happening right now?' said Annie.

"C is finding out the awful but obvious truth that J there is a dumb hot. A handsome idiot. A beautiful moron," said A.

"Oh. Sads. He's still a hot though," said Annie.

"Totally a hot," A agreed.

In Jonathan's car, he pointed over his shoulder. His biceps flexed against the fabric of his shirt, which made it hard for C to hear him.

"I can drive if you want. It's just we're going to the Sizzler."

It dawned on C what the cause of the confusion was here. "Right. Cool. Yeah, we can just walk."

Jonathan got out of the car and ran around to open her door and help her out. Again, he looked away, which she appreciated. Everything down there was out for the world to see.

"I want William to open a door like that for *me*. Where *is* he?" said Annie. A crinkled her nose at hearing her calling him 'William' like that was his real name or something. Hadn't he wanted to meet them here for his crusty old dude business? He'd better have gotten a costume.

"He'll be around here somewhere. There's nowhere else to go in this town. I have his Dad's Blockbuster card."

Back inside the V-Mart, B exited from the storeroom and found himself locking eyes with Mrs K. She was in her usual spot, reading a magazine that claimed Elvis was alive and fighting the Sandinista for Ronald Reagan, who was secretly still president.

They both froze, not expecting to see each other.

"Billy, what are you doing in my storeroom?" She always called him Billy.

Billy considered lying to her, but figured it was best to lay it all out. Maybe she would believe him.

"I'm helping some old dead dudes stuck in a Big Suck to get their magic dagger so they can get their bodies back that they lost to a demon or god or something."

Mrs K put down her magazine and motioned him over to the office.

She swung it open to reveal The Teeth sitting on her office desk.

Horn Teeth and Gap Teeth were wrestling each other. The others seemed to be placing bets with paperclips. Head Teeth turned and, seeing Mrs K, smiled at her.

"Something weird is going on tonight," she said to Billy.

Billy felt a wave of relief that someone believed him. These strange creatures must be a part of it. They looked like a Critter had mated with a Carebear that was very interested in dentistry. All day, he had felt like he was trying to do a puzzle without the picture on the box or staring at a *Where's Waldo?* that didn't have a goddamn Waldo in it.

"Something strange is afoot," he said.

Behind them, the Big Suck machine made a strange gurgling noise. Then they heard Giles and Augustus chanting in Latin.

Mrs K closed the door to the office, leaving The Teeth to their vices.

"What's that sound?" she asked.

"That's the crusty dudes. They're inside the machine, incanting," said B.

On top of the machine, where the frozen liquid was mixed, the frosty cola glowed red and blue as the machine vibrated and rocked.

"We have attained mass. Pull the lever! Release us!" came Giles' voice, muffled from inside the machine.

B looked at Mrs K, who nodded at him.

"PULL THE LEVER, CRETIN!" yelled Giles. B ran over and opened the handle slowly. Air spluttered out and then frozen sludge flowed into the cup. They watched as the orbs squeezed and elongated to pass through the tap.

"I don't like this," said Giles, his voice distorted.

"Stop complaining, Giles. Do the transmogrify spell quickly, before we overflow!" said Augustus, with rare urgency in his voice.

Giles incanted in Latin again as they poured back into the cup and retook their shape as orbs. The cup itself began to magically deform and grow, expanding beyond its normal shape. The cup bulged to accommodate the massive new volume of liquid as the plastic flowed like molten glass and gravity pulled it over the tray to the floor. The cup started to take on an unnatural form as the air crackled with arcane magic.

B and Mrs K stared in awe.

"You should go get everyone. We can stay in here until whatever else is happening tonight goes away," said Mrs K.

"Right on, Mrs K."

Mrs K was no coward, but she saw no reason to put herself and her kids in danger. She'd get these crusty old dudes outside and the kids inside. This thing could find its own manor and dagger or whatever the hell it was after. She and the kids would be safe in the V-Mart. Years of reading tabloids about all manner of satanic and occult occurrences across the entire country had steeled in her mind the idea that it was generally best not to get involved with witchcraft.

"Take them with you and maybe ditch them if you get the chance. I'm going to ask the *dokkaebi* what the hell is going on."

16

The Chad Baxter Problem

Annie had found a cleanish piece of cardboard so she could sit on the curb next to A. A wasn't sure how she felt about this, but she supposed it was better than her standing. People might have seen her from the road if she'd been upright and stopped to check what they were seeing. A did not need that. She was finally getting what she wanted. Mostly. It was Halloween, and she had a costume. No friends, but surely they would come crawling back any second now, C from her lame dumb date and B admitting to his bullshit story. Little did she know…

"So this is what you guys do just, like, hang out here?" asked Annie.

A lit another smoke.

"Yeah. I mean sometimes we stand, and there are usually more of me. I mean us. B and C sit there," she said, vaguely pointing.

"It's fun."

"Don't lie."

"I'm bored."

"Now you're getting it. Let it steal your hopes and dreams."

The V-Mart doors dinged open and B ran out to the curb. Annie jumped up with a squeal and hugged him. A remained sitting but turned her head ready for an apology, both for his bullshit as well as for not getting a costume.

"Where have you been, babe? Where's your costume?" Annie asked.

Behind him, the V-Mart doors began to close, but before they could, shuffling like a baby just learning to walk came a human sized Monster Big Suck cup deformed into a homunculus in the shape of the V-Mart's cartoon mascot Count Suckula. Inside its head floated the twin orbs of Giles and Augustus. It got caught by the closing door and had to shove its way out.

"Take heed, brother, we can still spill," said Giles, his orb glowing as he spoke.

A stood slowly, her cigarette falling out of her mouth. What was she looking at?

"Shoosh, brother. We are in the company of great beauty," said Augustus.

Annie blushed as The Count bowed to her, placing a hand over the opening at the top of its head to prevent spillage. It straightened, took her hand and lifted it to its plastic two-dimensional vampire mouth to mock kiss. The mouth did not move, but it was cold and wet from condensation.

"Hey, that's my girlfriend." said B.

The Count ignored him. It tried to take A's hand and she slapped it away.

"NO!" she yelled at the kiss and this thing's very existence.

Annie was beaming at B.

"Girlfriend?" she asked, raising a perfectly plucked eyebrow.

"Yeah?" said B, unsure.

"Okay."

B kissed her quickly so she couldn't take it back.

A wanted answers and was sick of waiting.

"WHY IS THIS THING?" she yelled at B.

"This is the old dudes. Giles and Gus. We have to find their dagger so they go away," said B. A threw up her hands and walked away. She stopped and looked back at the thing. It was *real*. She couldn't believe it.

"I still don't believe you," she said. They were all staring at The Count.

"Yeah, I get it. Where's C?" asked B.

A pointed without looking at the Sizzler, unable to take her eyes off the walking, talking vampire mascot cup thing standing on *her* curb.

"We have to go get her so she can figure this all out," said B.

B took Annie's hand and they started to cross the lot.

A came back to the curb and picked up her cigarette. She took a drag and then flicked it at The Count before following B and Annie, dragging her feet. She looked back and saw The Count following them. A did not like this at all and feared she had somehow conjured it up out of her desire for *something* to happen. She decided she would never want anything again.

The Count didn't notice. The orbs were like eyes following Annie's every step.

"Brother, that beguiling creature is terribly familiar," whispered Augustus.

"She would be to you, you fiend," whispered back Giles.

"Oh, dear brother."

"Got it, have you?"

"She is the image of our virgin, back from the dead."

Chad Baxter, eighteen, high school senior asshole and junior senior assistant Sizzler co-manager, scowled as B, A, Annie and an old pervert guy dressed like a shitty Dracula approached the hospitality desk. He'd seen them walking across the street and was ready for them.

B tried to blow past him, "Hey, Chad Baxter, we'll be two minutes, we're just here to grab our friend…"

Chad Baxter held his hand up like a stop sign and stepped out from behind his post to block the way.

"No. You have to order to enter," he said.

"'No', Chad Baxter?" asked B.

"Yes, I said 'no,'" said Chad Baxter.

"I'll show you 'no,' Chad Baxter," said A, getting into his face. B had to hold her back.

"Our new All You Can Eat Shrimp & Salad Bar is $7.99 each. Times four is $31.96," said Chad Baxter.

B pulled his wallet chain from his jeans pocket and opened his beat up Velcro Hardy Boys wallet. He had almost twenty bucks. $19.25 to be exact. He looked at A, who gestured to her lack of pockets. He looked to The Count, who was still staring at Annie. That felt like a problem for later. Annie also had no pockets.

"Okay. What about two adults and two children under twelve for free, Chad Baxter?" B said, pointing at A and The Count.

"Nope. $31.96. You assholes use my whole name. You pay the whole price."

"You will rue this day, Chad Baxter," said A, poking him in the chest.

Chad Baxter smirked at her. Chad Baxter was six feet tall. Chad Baxter wore black frame glasses. Chad Baxter had greasy black hair slicked back. Chad Baxter's Sizzler uniform of dress pants and a polo shirt tucked in made him look like an old man who enjoyed pottering around the garden and golfing. It was not a good look on him.

"I rue you, freak," he said to A.

It wasn't nearly as clever as it had sounded in his head.

17

Showtime in Underwood

As the last light of the day blinked out behind the ridge of the valley, Underwood's Main Street was comparatively busy. Two dozen or so kids and teens were trick or treating, and the few operating stores had stayed open an extra half hour, hoping that having a bowl of free candy on their counters would improve business. It didn't. Most of the adults who were on chaperon duty stayed standing outside drinking cheap wine from 7-Eleven Big Gulp cups as their kids ran in, snatched whatever candy they could and ran out again. The real Halloween action in Underwood was going on in the hills, where kids, both rich and poor, mingled on the woody streets lined with big houses that had the best candy. No one really tricked or treated in the poor parts of town, which was most of the rest of town.

One parent, Cynthia Rhodes, in leopard print leggings, pink shoulder-padded leather jacket and big hair, chewed gum as she waited for her little shit Zachery to get his candy from the liquor store. She was about to yell at Zach to hurry the heck up when she felt a rumble. She turned to watch another parent grab her daughter out of the middle of the street to avoid being flattened like a pancake by a fleet of vans, open-top jeeps, box trucks, semi-trailers and heavy equipment speeding down the street in a convoy.

All were marked with the V-Mart logo and passed quickly down Main Street towards the V-Mart intersection. They entered the lot and formed a loose half-circle around the front of the store, blocking the entry and exit driveways. They filled the lot. The semi-trailers parked on Woodhill Street between the V-Mart and the empty lot, blocking it completely.

Out of the vehicles poured almost a hundred men and women. There were Scientists in V-Mart lab coats, Occultists with the V-Mart logo embroidered on their black robes, Muscled Goons in tight V-Mart polo shirts or V-Mart branded boiler suits. They all moved with purpose. Each person knew their role. They unloaded computer equipment, large magnetic tape arrays, CRT monitoring devices and strange occultist ritual items.

Boiler-suited Goons placed large square silver boxes at intervals around the lot between the equipment. They unlocked them with a satisfying click. The tops of the cases popped open, the sides folded down and from inside sprung up portable work lights on Meccano-like stands. They lit the lot in a sodium-yellow vapor glow that clashed with the blue hour light to create a strange greenish vibe.

The V-Mart Tech Goons dragged long looms of SCART cables and plugged a bank of computers into the tape arrays and then into the CRT monitors and finally into the control center inside one of the semi-trailers that was filled with workstations right out of *War Games.* Other Goons ran power from a pit near the front of the store.

The computers booted up and the inside of the trailer glowed in CRT green.

A particularly muscle-bound Goon in V-Mart overalls with no shirt underneath, whose bulging chest, arms and back made Jonathan look like a puny baby man, opened a black V-Mart logo emblazoned tool chest and took out a gigantic jackhammer. Everyone called him Jackhammer Guy, even those who knew his name.

All over the lot, large boxy walkie-talkie radios squawked to life.

"Goddess inbound," said a voice. All movement on the lot stopped.

The V-Mart employees waited.

A decked-out RV roared down Main Street. It screeched into the lot and took prime position on the inside of the circle of work vehicles. It had barely come to a halt before the side door opened. Out stepped Killian Vass. She was dressed to kill in a pure white pencil dress. Gina and Tiffany emerged behind her.

Killian took a moment to take in the scene. She looked several of her V-Mart acolytes in the eye as she strode into the center of the half circle and looked at the store. She hated that her empire was nothing but a chain of these things. Tonight, she was going to change that. She had grand designs to reshape Vass Enterprises into the "it" brand of the 1990s.

She was ready.

This was the moment.

She wanted them all to feel it like she did.

She deliberately paused.

She looked up at the sky and the stars, even though they were mostly washed out by the lighting.

She looked down at the ground slowly so that they could follow her gaze.

This was the place.

This was *the* spot.

She knelt sideways so as not to expose herself given the tightness of her outfit. She'd actually practiced how to get herself in the right position. With an expression of distaste, she picked up a discarded cigarette butt and dropped it into Tiffany's now waiting hand. Gina swept in and handed her a can of hot pink spray paint.

Killian sprayed a large "K" on the ground. She stood and tossed the can back to Gina, smiling and giving a little nod to no one and everyone as she walked inside the store.

Jackhammer Guy, standing at the edge of the waiting circle, walked forward to the middle of the 'K'. He powered up his monster rig and started to excavate.

Mrs K was sitting at her desk with a shotgun resting on her lap. The store had never been robbed, but she insisted it was always loaded and locked in the office just in case.

On the desk, Head Teeth was gesturing wildly and chatting away. These things spoke an old-fashioned Korean dialect. Mrs K understood enough that she could piece it together if she filtered out the words that made no sense and ignored how the teeth chattering changed the sound of certain letters.

The Teeth, as they called themselves, were quite intriguing. They thought of themselves entirely in the singular as a collective but each had unique a personality and often contradictory politics.

Mrs K had found out that they shared a single cultural memory and consciousness. If one knew something, they all knew something. Head Teeth seemed to be their leader, but only through the force of its will. If they had ever been like her father's *dokkaebi*, it must have been thousands of years ago, and they were now something different. They had told her that this was how long they had served The Great Maw. Mrs K was concerned about this but unsure what she could do about it from her office. They had told her that The Maw had enslaved them and interbred them to suit its needs. It had done this even though they didn't appear to have defined genders, although Mrs K wasn't about to inquire about their bits and pieces.

She liked them and they liked her. It was instinctual for her to want to mother them like she did the kids who hung out at her store, although at first she'd questioned her instinct. She'd asked The Teeth if they wanted anything to eat, and they'd answered that they wanted teeth. It had taken her a little while to figure out they weren't cannibals and they wanted to eat *actual* teeth, human or otherwise, and not each other. Actual teeth seemed to hold value as currency to them. She'd given them some Doritos instead. They'd been briefly annoyed but ate them anyway.

For the last twenty minutes, they had been telling her about life on the other side of the sky hole they had traveled through. They'd come from a land of hard rocks and they lived underground in lava tubes where teeth as food were few and far between. Mrs K thought it sounded awful. The Teeth had been in charge of guarding souls that had been harvested by The Maw. It had collected millions of souls in a length of time beyond a human mind's understanding of the universe. Mrs K's head hurt. It was a lot of new information to absorb and it challenged most of her and the human race's understanding of life. Despite this, she felt equipped to keep trying. This is where her love of trashy tabloid magazines had paid off. She'd read about a lot of strange shit.

The topic of conversation now shifted to the terms of their enslavement. Perhaps unsurprisingly, The Teeth were deeply unhappy. They liked their work, but for hundreds of years The Maw had broken its promises to free them. The Teeth were starting to suspect The Maw was lying to them. All they wanted was their freedom. They'd keep working for The Maw. After all, it was all they knew. But they wanted to be paid. In *teeth*. They wanted her opinion.

"I think you know what you need to do. You need to *unionize*," she said in Korean (*nodongjohap-hwahada* is actually how she put it.) "Enforce your rights against this Grand Maw."

Head Teeth chattered back at her angrily.

"Sorry. *Great* Maw. Your Korean is old fashioned. My point still stands."

Head Teeth nodded and turned to the others. "See, this is what I've been telling you." It turned back to Mrs K, but she held up her hand to stop it winding up again. They were chatty little things, but something had startled her.

"What's that noise?" she said, now speaking English.

It sounded like a jackhammer.

18

Free Cheese Bread and the End of the World

A 'd had enough of Chad Baxter.

"COURTNEY! CHAD BAXTER IS BEING AN ASSHOLE!"

She pushed past him into the restaurant. The Sizzler was empty except for C, Jonathan and now B, A, Annie, The Count and an enraged Chad Baxter.

"Come back or I'll kick all your asses!" he yelled, chasing them.

The Count swiftly kicked Chad Baxter in the shins and, in the exact opposite expression, threw up its hands like it didn't mean to do it. Internally, there was some confusion about how this Count thing was controlled and which one of the brothers was doing the controlling.

"Nobody ever wins a batty fang, Chad Baxter," said Augustus. He had decided to de-modernize some of Dalton's sayings to make them more palatable to his own ear.

"What are you doing, brother? Maybe I should be in charge of our ambulation," said Giles.

"Relax, brother. You're doing great with our arms."

Jonathan had picked the best booth. It overlooked the intersection and the V-Mart. C had three plates stacked with every type of food on offer and an entire bowlful of bacon bits. Jonathan had gone straight for the ice cream and the soup. He hadn't yet touched either, wanting to finish his kids' puzzle mat first. He'd smashed the maze but was now stumped on the word finder. Tragically, they had already eaten all of the free cheese bread and Chad Baxter would bring no more. "Company policy," Chad Baxter had said.

Jonathan was watching the commotion across the street.

"Mom said head office was visiting, so it's probably just that."

C was thankful to see her friends rushing to her table. Jonathan wasn't getting *any* of her references. All he knew about was wrestling, cars and gym stuff. His musical taste was a disaster. He loved top one hundred slop like New Kids On The Block and Roxette. C assumed he'd been dancing to it ironically. She'd even had to explain to him what ironic meant. C had also started to wonder if physical attraction was more important than relating to each other intellectually.

"What's up?" she asked as the group reached the booth.

"I was wrong," A said. "B found old men in a cup. They can walk now."

She pointed at The Count. Augustus obliged by operating the legs so it stepped forward. C dropped her fork.

"I am Augustus Vass the third. I'm sharing this tonic with my brother Giles Vass the fourth…"

"I can speak for myself, brother," interrupted Giles.

"I don't… Okay. I'm Courtney," said C.

"We shouldn't confuse these good people, Giles. I will do all the talking from now on. You just work the hands," said

Augustus.

"They argue a lot," said B to C, as if that explained *anything* that was happening right now.

Jonathan turned back from the window.

"Yo, are you the *real* Count Suckula?" He was pumped, but everyone ignored him.

Giles took Augustus' advice literally. The Count slapped himself in the face.

"You're right, brother," said Giles. "I'll do this with the hands, will I?"

The Count slapped himself again.

The Count stumbled as the brothers fought for control inside the cup.

"Judas!" yelled Augustus.

"Judas, me?! You betrayed our sacred order for a piece of crumpet!"

"And I'd do it again!" Augustus shouted as Giles continued slapping.

19

Inventory

Still holding the shotgun, Mrs K opened her office door and looked out to see an overdressed woman standing in her store watching MTV with her back to her. Not wanting to cause a scare, she placed the gun against the inside wall of the office, closed the door softly and moved behind the counter.

"Sorry, we're closed," she said loudly.

Killian Vass turned and smiled, although the smile never reached her eyes. Mrs K waited for the woman to speak, but she said nothing. The woman was off putting, and Mrs K had no time for any more weirdness tonight.

"I love your outfit. We are doing inventory tonight. You'll have to come back later."

Killian spun in place at the compliment.

"Thank you. Mrs Kang, I presume?" said Killian. Mrs K nodded, taken aback that the woman knew her name. It never occurred to her that she was from head office. V-Mart only ever sent pale old white guys.

"I'm Killian Vass from head office. I'm the newly appointed lifetime CEO of Vass Enterprises," she said, adding quietly to herself, "…and of the world."

Mrs K looked out the windows and now noticed all the V-Mart vehicles and staff in the lot. She started walking towards Killian.

"Good. I don't know what it is you think you're here for or why you'd come on Halloween but I have a hole in my storeroom roof you need to send someone to fix right away."

Mrs K was on a roll and didn't hear the automatic doors ding open as two V-Mart Goons in boiler suits entered the store.

"And I need to talk to someone about why I wasn't invited to the shareholder meeting. Is my stock printed on toilet paper, hmm? Stacy Yuan, who runs the 7-Eleven, has convinced the Coke-a-Cola delivery man to only deliver me NEW COKE! No one wants that. What are you going to do about that!?"

Killian laughed.

"You *are* a pistol, Mrs Kang. Newsflash. You're out. Vass Enterprises has decided to make this a company-owned store. You'll receive a generous payout for the trouble and I'll personally buy back your stock. We need you to leave the property immediately. I'll have your personal effects sent on."

Mrs K's eyes widened in shock. She gave Killian a proper once over, and saw the Power Glove for the first time. She looked Killian right in the eyes.

"Like hell I'm leaving. This is about The Maw."

Killian dropped her smile.

"Take her. Find out how and how much she knows," she said.

The V-Mart Goons grabbed Mrs K under the arms and lifted her. She fought back like hell.

20

Road House Blues

In the Sizzler, Augustus was explaining the plot of *Road House* to Chad Baxter, who hadn't seen it, as a rationale for his behavior. The others were jammed into the booth and were trying to figure out what the hell was going on tonight.

"Is this my fault?" asked A. "I had no expectation this Halloween would be so ethically challenging. I just wanted to get dressed up."

B shook his head, even though he thought it probably was quite a lot her fault. C backed him up.

"No. You're fine. I'm not sure why we should help them," said C, gesturing to The Count.

"They're very convincing. They talk and talk until you agree with them," said B.

"I'm sure they are. They've convinced Chad Baxter of something," said C.

A, B, and Annie looked over to where Chad Baxter was demonstrating some Karate to The Count, who tried to front kick, spilling some of its liquid onto a nearby table.

"Mom…?" said Jonathan, almost in a whimper.

They turned back to the window. Across the street they caught a glimpse between vehicles of Mrs K fighting tooth and nail as now *four* Goons dragged her somewhere beyond their view.

"Chad Baxter, call the cops!" yelled C.

"What?" asked Chad Baxter. He'd been describing the concept of 'chi' to the guys in the vampire costume. He wasn't sure why they were both sharing one costume.

"CHAD BAXTER, CALL THE COPS!" screamed A at the top of her tiny lungs.

For once in his asshole life, Chad Baxter did what he was told.

21

Party Town

Funky Cold Medina by Tone-Loc was playing on MTV in the V-Mart. It was also blasting from the PA speakers mounted on Killian's RV. The RV was her lair away from home. Inside, she had a stack of TVs also tuned to MTV. One wall of the RV was a two-way mirror so she could watch her people work as she reclined in a custom pink leather La-Z-Boy reading *Art of the Deal* and laughing her ass off. What a load of bullshit, she thought. She tore a page out and handed it to Gina to read, who was pacing nervously back and forth over the RV's pure white carpet.

The V-Mart Goons were tearing up the lot where Killian's 'K' had marked the spot. Jackhammer Guy's bi's, tri's and chest all pumped in time to the music as he worked to break up the layer of concrete beneath the lot's asphalt that he and his crew of other jackhammer guys, none as buff as him, had already cleared. V-Mart Scientists bopped to the music as they continued setting up their high-tech racks of computers and custom black magic measuring equipment. In the control center semi-trailer, the V-Mart Techs typed on their keyboards in rhythm to the music, running software that filled their CRT screens in green code that gave the trailer an almost radioactive vibe. A backhoe dumped concrete from the cleared sections of the lot right onto Main Street, almost hitting a passing car. No care at all was given to public safety. V-Mart's OH&S team had not been invited to tonight's operation.

Jackhammer Guy abruptly shuddered and lurched forward as his jackhammer hit open air beneath the lot's concrete base. He whistled loudly over the music and waved his giant arms to get a V-Mart Occultists attention. The Occultist rushed over with a powerful flashlight as Jackhammer Guy enlarged the hole. He moved back as the Occultist stuck his head into the hole, shining the flashlight inside.

Holy shit.

They had hit pay dirt.

In the dark beneath the lot, the beam of light illuminated wall-to-wall wooden bookshelves. They were filled with moldy books, dirty scrolls and occult objects in various states of decay. The Occultist swept the light across the space and saw a dusty black marble altar inlaid with gold occult symbols. He lifted himself back up and nodded to Tiffany, who had joined him near the hole. She lifted her walkie-talkie to her mouth.

"We've found it!"

Her voice was broadcast across the lot via the RV's PA system. The V-Mart staff cheered in unison. Inside the RV, Killian giggled and danced like she did not give a fuck if anyone was watching.

Chad Baxter rushed over to the booth, breathless. He'd called the cops from the phone in the kitchen. The kitchen staff had left as soon as they'd heard there was trouble. Usually, most of them pretended not to speak English so they could ignore Chad Baxter. Tonight, the lie wasn't worth the effort. The busboys had also fled, and now Chad Baxter was a man alone in charge of his Sizzler. There were many like it, but this one was his.

A, B, C, Annie, Jonathan and The Count were transfixed at the window like it was *Can't Miss TV*. They were trying to see what was happening on the lot and where these V-Mart assholes had taken their Mrs K.

"The cops are on their way. I told them it was terrorists like in *Die Hard*," Chad Baxter said.

A stood up from the booth and rounded on The Count.

"This is all because of you!"

The Count's hands went up defensively.

"Surely not," said Augustus.

"How dare you!" said Giles.

"Hold on, *what* are you saying we did? I don't want to miss out on being praised if we *did* do something," said Augustus.

A wasn't precisely sure what she *was* accusing them of.

"I don't know, but I just know it's your fault," she said. "It *has* to be."

Jonathan was stirring one of his bowls of ice cream into a thick shake. He felt powerless and was eating his feelings. C'd had to convince him to stay in the Sizzler until they knew what was going on. She felt sorry for him. He was still sweet even if they had nothing in common, although he did still have those arms and chest and…

"Maybe they want the tiny cat demons?" Jonathan said, taking a long swig of his bowl.

"Cat demons?" C asked.

Jonathan opened his mouth to explain, but it was still full of melted ice cream. He quickly swallowed, but a large amount of thick goop still escaped, covering his chiseled chin.

A and Annie shared a look. A nodded and mouthed, "So dumb."

Annie mouthed, "So hot," back. A had to cover her mouth not to laugh. She caught herself. Am I making jokes with *Annie Munro*? Her train of thought was interrupted by B.

"Yeah, there are cat demons. Tiny monsters with big teeth. Mrs K has them in her office. And they love her."

The Teeth were taking a vote about whether to go on strike. They knew this would not make The Maw very happy. To pass, they all had to agree. Head Teeth counted the raised paws. Even though the Teeth all knew each other's thoughts, Head Teeth was big on doing things the right way.

Bat Teeth was the lone holdout, so the motion failed.

Again.

Head Teeth gnashed its teeth at Bat Teeth.

Bat Teeth chattered its teeth back in a way they knew meant, "All hail the Great Maw."

Head Teeth shared a thought with the others.

Bat Teeth had no time to react as they pounced, tearing it apart and dividing its teeth amongst themselves equally.

It was quick and gruesome, but in order to preserve Teeth unity, it had to be done.

Head Teeth proposed the strike motion once more.

This time the vote passed unanimously.

"Oh dear, The Teeth, brother. We're running out of time," panicked Giles. A pointed.

"See. It's *them*. Get them," she said to C.

C grabbed The Count. She was stronger and faster than she looked. In fact, during freshman year, Coach Turner had convinced Courtney to join the girls' basketball team based on her height. At fourteen, she was taller than most seniors. She'd only lasted one game after breaking an opposing player's nose by passing the ball to her face. Courtney had claimed ignorance about the rules of a 'sport' and had assumed she was able to use the ball this way. The girl had called her a bad name, and Courtney didn't take shit from anyone, and further violence had ensued. It had been a while since anyone else had given her shit. Like the other weirds, she was ignored by most of the other kids at Underwood High.

Now she slammed this possessed frozen-sludge *thing* into the nearest wall, surprising it with her force. Some of the Big Suck splashed out and dripped down its grinning vampire face. Inside its head, the orbs sloshed around violently.

"It's time for answers! Why did those people take Mr K? Why are they digging up our favorite car park? What are The Teeth? And why do you really want this so-called magical dagger?" she said coldly as her blood boiled.

Jonathan was impressed by her strength-to-weight ratio. He, too, had been worried they had nothing in common, but maybe he'd be able to show her the glory of lifting heavy things repeatedly after all. He went to look her up and down but got stuck on her long legs…

"I'd love to explain, but as a woman, this may be too complex for…" Giles attempted to say.

C slammed his plastic head hard against the wall again, and more of its contents splashed on the wall, as well as on a pastoral print of cows in a field. Sizzler loved a pastoral print decoration.

You could have one, too, for the low price of $29.99 plus tax.

Chad Baxter thought about complaining about the destruction of fine art and Sizzler property, but A looked at him and he shut up before saying anything, thinking better of it.

Annie clapped.

"This is *so* much better than Sasha Gillespie's Stupid Biannual Blow Job & Pool Party."

B shook his head. He didn't want to know, but was *kind* of interested. If Annie had done that with other people, would she do it with him?

"Careful, brother, you've angered the Amazonian. Let me. I've always been better with the fairer sex," said Augustus. The Count never saw it coming. Its plastic face made a popping sound as the nose cracked under the force of C jabbing it. She held her fist up and shook it to let them know she had plenty more left. In shock, the brothers spilled their guts, rapidly talking over each other.

"We don't know who those people are!" said Giles.

"Or why they're digging," followed Augustus.

"The Teeth are servants of the Great Maw, an ancient demon beyond human understanding."

"The dagger is for a ritual we need to do so The Maw does not devour us."

"Again…"

"And the ritual is to get your bodies back?" asked B, trying to hurry them along.

"That would certainly be an auxiliary benefit," said Giles.

"What would be the *non*-auxiliary benefit?" asked A.

The Count said nothing. The orbs backed away from the front of the cup to confer.

"Spill these jerks," said A to C.

C pulled The Count away from the wall and forced it sideways. Inside the Big Suck, the liquid slanted towards the cup's open top. The orbs bobbed in the half-frozen liquid, dangerously close to the opening.

"No, no, wait! Give us one moment," begged Giles.

"I believe they have reached the part where it is time for them to not to be nice, brother," said Augustus.

"The ritual invokes the demon: The Great Maw," said Giles. C straightened The Count slightly, but not yet all the way upright. The threat of decanting the brothers onto the dirty Sizzler's patterned carpet still remained.

"Invocation usually makes him quite mad. Demons hate being invoked," said Augustus.

"That's why we need to complete the ritual before midnight on Halloween."

"Those are like his business hours. At midnight, we'll have to wait another year."

"Also, in order to gain his favor we must appease him with the blood of a virgin sacrifice, which will make him amenable to striking a bargain," said Giles.

"*Oh no!*" thought everyone in the Sizzler. This *wasn't* just two old guys' souls embodying a magical plastic cup shaped like a vampire mascot. Chad Baxter became so confused he started wondering if the Sizzler Corporation of America negotiated with terrorists. For the record their official policy, filed in a secret folder locked in a safe that also contains the secret recipe for the cheese bread, deep inside their corporate headquarters thousands of miles away, was that staff are expendable.

"Once invoked, The Maw will help us shape the world as we see fit. We just need our magical dagger for the virgin, and the manor because it has our favorite altar. I suppose we could use someone else's altar in a pinch, but it never feels quite the same," said Augustus.

"Of course we're going to use *our* altar. Not to do so would be scandalous." Giles scoffed.

"Frankly, the idea of someone else's altar sickens me, but I suppose we could have a maid wash it first," Augustus said.

C let go of The Count as she and the others reeled from these douche bag's explanations. She slumped back into the booth with a deep sigh. This was it, then.

"Fuck," said B. He could not believe he'd trusted them.

"Fuck," said C. She'd told B these dudes were trouble.

"FUCK!" said A. She had just wanted a nice Halloween.

Annie put her hand on B's shoulder as he, too, slumped back into the booth.

"I've been helping the bad guys," he said into his hands.

"How can *we* be the bad guys? We're just trying to rule the world," reasoned Augustus.

Giles really had had enough of these poor children and their inane questions.

"I can see you're vexed. Just point us towards our manor and I'm sure we can sort the rest out ourselves," he said.

They all looked at The Count blankly.

"This town doesn't have a manor," said Annie.

"It has nothing," said C.

"Except our V-Mart," said A.

"And the burnt out husk of a Bubble Gum factory," said B.

With a mouth still full of melted ice cream, Jonathan mumbled.

"The manor is the V-Mart."

The microwave in the V-Mart beeped and a hungry V-Mart

Goon in a polo shirt opened the door to pull out a lava-hot burrito. He took a bite that burnt his whole mouth. He felt blisters form on his tongue. He huffed with his open mouth, trying to cool it enough to swallow. Screwed to the wall next to the microwave was a framed photo and a plaque that no one except Jonathan, who cleaned it every few days, had ever looked at or read. Not even Mrs K knew it was there. The old sepia-toned picture showed an annoyed by how-long-is-this-photograph-thing-going-to-take Giles and Augustus standing next to their exhausted looking wives and blurry children who had refused to stay still. They were positioned in front of a large Victorian-era manor. The accompanying plaque read:

This V-Mart stands on the site of Vass Manor, destroyed by fire in 1904 due to the personal misuse of the world's first electrical outlet by Octavian (Otto) Vass II.

"This means that the V-People out there want the same thing as the Big Suck dudes," said C. V-People didn't sound right to her, so she started rewriting it in her head.

"To rule the world," said B.

"*And* ruin our Halloween," said A.

They were scared. This wasn't just going to ruin Halloween. It could ruin *everything*. Their whole lives. What would happen to them without the V-Mart and their curb?

Augustus was thrilled that they all seemed to be getting how important this was. He was not reading the room.

"You'll still help us then?" he asked.

"I showed you guys *Road House* even though it was overdue, and you betrayed me," said B.

C was was ready to do violence again. She balled her fists

so hard her knuckles cracked like gunshots in the empty restaurant.

Augustus finally realized the tenor of the room had turned against them.

"Perhaps as a form of apology, you'd all like to join our secret coven?" he asked.

"Well, not the *women,* of course," Giles clarified.

"No. No. Although they could certainly take part in the occasional private magic tuition," Augustus said, leering The Count's cheesy vampire face at Annie. "Actually, I think we may have once sacrificed a relative of yours. She was quite the 'babe,' as you kids say."

"Gross," said Annie. At the back of her mind she remembered the first time she'd come home with a hickey on her neck at age fifteen. Her father had said nothing and avoided eye contact with her until it had faded. Her mother, on the other hand, had taken to muttering about Annie ending up like her great great great Aunt Stephanie. This memory now clicked with another one. Her great grandmother, drunk one Thanksgiving when Annie was ten, threatening to spill the family's dark secrets regarding a satanic cult. No one knew what she was going on about. Now Annie knew she was right. These cup dudes had killed Aunt Stephanie in their stupid ritual. She had been their virgin.

C looked at the lurking Chad Baxter. "Chad Baxter, please escort Count Suckula here from the Sizzler," she said through gritted teeth.

"Why should I? You still owe me $31.96," he said, sulking and crossing his arms.

"You saw what she can do, Chad Baxter. Don't test us," said A.

Chad Baxter thought about it for a second and then put a hand on The Count's shoulder. He wasn't doing it because it was the right thing, but because he loved power, and right now, this was the only power he had left.

"Sir, with the power invested in me as junior senior co-manager by the Sizzler Corporation of America, I must ask you to leave the premises. Sorry, she scares me," he added.

"Well," said Augustus.

"I see," said Giles.

"You too, Chad Baxter. We are commandeering this Sizzler," said A.

He started to protest, but she cut him off.

"GET. THE FUCK. OUT!"

Chad Baxter got. The fuck. Out.

22

The Living Tempest

The Count and Chad Baxter stepped out of the Sizzler and into the night. B locked the doors as they walked away. Giles took a moment to wipe the spilled liquid from The Count's face and gingerly tested the fragility of the crack that woman had caused in the nose. It seemed like it would hold, at least for now. Giles searched his mind for a spell that might repair it, but came up empty. Augustus, meanwhile, had other priorities.

"Well, I suppose we should go introduce ourselves to our relative," he said, optimistically.

"Honestly, I wish we'd known about him sooner. We wouldn't have had to deal with that miscreant and his harem," said Giles excitedly.

"You always were too trusting, brother. Come, Chad Baxter, you shall make us an excellent body man. I shall teach you the ways of Dalton, and you shall instruct us on the customs of the nineteen hundred and eighties," said Augustus. Chad Baxter didn't know what a body man was, but joined them anyway. The three men in two bodies walked across the Sizzler car park

109

towards the intersection.

The sound of sirens was coming closer. On the V-Mart lot, Killian's crew had uncovered the vast occult library of the former Vass Manor hidden for almost a hundred years beneath the car park. The pit they had dug out was now ten feet deep and twice as wide, and matched the vaguely circular shape of the room below. There were two doorways blocked with debris that surely led into whatever else remained of the basement that had hidden the Vass family's love of the occult from polite society. For now, they remained undisturbed. The V-Mart Goons had assembled a scaffold stairway that zigzagged down into the library. Goons worked hard and fast. They were emptying the library of the rubble, dust and skeletal human remains of the last failed attempt at the ritual. In the center stood the marble altar where Stephanie Munro had taken her last breath. Goons were now scrubbing and polishing it along with the marble floor and its inlaid gold symbols.

A Scientist approached the altar. With a custom-built bolt gun he clamped electronic sensors on each end of the altar. They were connected via thick, woven cables to a monitoring station set up on carts at the rim of the pit. On a CRT screen, two dot matrix circles, one red and one green, overlapped slightly like a Venn diagram. Each circle flashed on and off, but out of time. A V-Mart Tech spoke into his walkie-talkie, "We have pulses. They are asymmetrical but moving towards alignment. We will be go for invocation in fifteen minutes. Repeat, we'll be go for invocation in fifteen." His words were broadcast over the RV's PA system. On the screen, the colored circles moved closer to overlapping each other with each pulse.

Jackhammer Guy, his work done, high-fived the rest of

his crew of other jackhammer guys and headed inside to get Monster Big Sucks for all the boys. He'd heard the new sour bubblegum flavor was the bomb.

Killian stood at the window of her RV watching everything. The library was real. It was here and it was beautiful. She, like Giles and Augustus, could not imagine using another altar. This hunk of black stone had been commissioned by the Vass family over four hundred years ago. It'd been quarried and shaped by the best stonemasons of their age into an altar like no other. Mind you, they'd never been paid for their work. The altar had originally been placed in a stone circle deep in the woods of the Black Forests of the Vass homeland. Its disassembly, transportation and reassembly in the New World was a family tale of legend. Killian's mother, a weak, submissive woman, had whispered the story to her as she drifted off to sleep as a child. It was Killian's only fond memory of her long dead mother. Truth be told, Killian loved the stone more than she had ever loved her mother. That dusty bitch could choke on Killian's success. The altar's powerful occult symbols were exactly as described in the surviving accounts of her useless male ancestors' failed invocation a hundred years ago tonight. This had been almost *too* easy.

On cue, a block down on Main Street, two cop cars flashing their lights now came into sight.

"Local law enforcement has responded as expected," said Gina.

"Have they now?" said Killian.

On the stack of TVs, a black and white music video started. A woman was running her hands over dark water. Killian gasped in joy. She felt full body chills and was overwhelmed by a wave of emotional euphoria. The French called this sensation *frisson.*

Not everyone experienced this intense reaction to music or art, however Killian was particularly sensitive to it. The timing of the song was impeccable.

"Pump it," she said,

She closed her eyes and listened to the first few notes as Gina turned the dial all the way up. The RV shook and vibrated from the bass as the song blasted through the PA.

This was Killian's favorite song from the soundtrack of her favorite movie.

It was *She's Like the Wind* by Patrick Swayze featuring Wendy Frazier from the *Dirty Dancing* soundtrack.

As Swayze began to sing, Killian melted inside and out. She held up the Power Glove. She flipped a switch and it whirred to life. She opened her eyes.

Above the V-Mart, clouds swirled in and obscured the stars, like they'd been summoned. In fact, they had been. Killian exited the RV as Swayze sang about his heart being taken. She strutted through the lot and toward the intersection as the two cop cars action movie slid to a stop in front of her. She was out of their league.

Four cops, three men and a woman, jumped out of their vehicles and from behind their doors pointed their guns at Killian.

"Freeze," yelled an older, rounder male cop.

Even out here on the street he was barely audible over the music.

He was a fool to believe Killian would stop for anyone.

She walked towards the cars as a handful of feet behind her, lightning struck the road with a crack and boom. The flash blinded the police, and a male rookie cop fired blindly in fear. Killian moved with the grace of a dancer, her hair whipping perfectly in the sudden rushing wind of the building storm. She swiped her gloved hand. The bullets changed direction and arc-ed into the palm of her glove, caught by its magnets. She closed her fist.

BOOM!

Lightning curved out of the sky into the glove. She opened her palm. The lightning and bullets shot out.

"This is insane," said the older cop right before lightning hit the car, and the bullets from his young partner's gun peppered the door. It was his last thought as the car exploded in flames and a shower of sparks. The older cop, along with his now also dead rookie partner, flew through the air in large chunky pieces of gore that splattered upon Main Street with dull wet thuds.

"Oh wow. Fun," said Killian as Swayze belted out the chorus to his US Billboard Hot 100 Number 3 hit. It had been Number 1 on the Billboard Adult Contemporary Chart, but who counted that? Certainly not Killian.

The Count and Chad Baxter were watching the drama unfold from the Sizzler corner of the intersection. If The Count had been able to open its mouth, it would have been agape in awe and terror. Chad Baxter peed a little, although not enough to notice on the dark fabric of his Sizzler issued dress pants.

"Who *is* she?" asked Giles over the racket these people called music.

"She is a living tempest. A siren. Listen Brother. Dalton sings for her!" replied Augustus. Not only was Dalton handsome, but he had the voice of an angel. Was there anything he couldn't do? If so, Augustus imagined he was a quick study like Augustus himself.

"What a babe!" yelled Chad Baxter to no one.

The last living male cop screamed into his radio for backup as he cowered behind his car door. It was like he could feel the gloved woman's breath on his neck.

The door he was hiding behind rocked abruptly before it was torn off its hinges with a metal scream. Killian, seven feet away, had pulled it loose violently with the power of the gloves' magnets. Before the door reached her she flicked her wrist and it spun around and flew back towards the car. The male cop stood and raised his hands in surrender. It did nothing. The door cut him cleanly in half. It sliced into the car and through the cop like he was deli meat. His legs stayed upright for a few seconds before they crumpled to the ground, spurting blood. His torso, still alive for a moment, slid down the door and joined his legs in a bloody mass of intestines and other internal organs as he died. It was gross.

The remaining cop sprinted down Main Street towards the lights of more cop cars coming up the street towards their doom.

Killian summoned more lightning into her glove and fired it at the cop just as she thought she'd gotten far enough away to be safe. The blast hit her in the middle of her back, lifting her into the air. She appeared to hang there for a moment as her flesh exploded off her bones and vaporized into red mist. Her skeleton clattered to the road like something out of a Saturday morning cartoon.

In the Sizzler, the gang saw it all happen from the large window overlooking the intersection. Killian's chaos reflected in the glass and across their faces.

"Again, when I stated earlier that I wanted something to happen tonight… this was not it," said A.

"Trick or treat ruined forever," said B. The two of them turned away from the window. Annie put her arms around B as he slumped, once more, into the booth.

C couldn't look away. She watched as half a dozen other cop cars arrived.

Killian went full Darth Vass.

Chaos. Death. Blood. Explosions. Skeletons. Melted pools of candle wax-like flesh.

The others couldn't watch.

C couldn't look away.

She saw everyone in town who could help them die while she stood there.

"How do we stop this?' said A, covering her ears to block out the screaming of those not yet totally dead.

"We could make a run for the border. They have V-Mart's in Mexico, right?" said B, "*Una Gran Chupada, por favor?*" Mrs Landry, their Spanish teacher, would've been proud.

"We could negotiate with the lightning lady. I could compliment her shoes," said Annie quietly, trying to lighten the mood.

"What's going to happen to my Mom?" said Jonathan.

They all looked at him.

Fuck. Mrs K.

Lightning struck outside repeatedly. Paramedics and Fire Engines arrived. Killian massacred these first responders too, just like the cops. The intersection was soon filled with abandoned and destroyed emergency vehicles on fire.

C turned to the others. When she spoke her voice was punctuated by booms of thunder.

"No," she said firmly. "No hiding. No negotiation. No *Gran Chupada*. That is *our* car park. *Our* Mrs K," she said.

"Our whole *world*. How do we save the *world*? We failed gym class," B pointed out.

"I hate the world. It's my least favorite place. It gets everywhere," shivered A.

"The world can sort itself out. We just have to save Mrs K," said C as she grabbed Jonathan's puzzle place mat. She flipped it over and quickly drew a map of the intersection, marking the V-Mart, Carpet King Lot, Sizzler and the Sporting Goods store with unsurprising detail given her drawing talent. The others all squished back into the booth as she drew, except for Jonathan who was already still slumped in it.

"We just have to get Mrs K back from these Vassholes and stop the ritual. Hold them off till midnight. Halloween business hours, remember?" she said. "If we can figure out where they're holding her, maybe we can grab her. Like, if we cause a distraction. It always works on *The Hardy Boys* and *Nancy Drew*."

B pointed to the Carpet King lot on her map, "If I climb the big oak tree on the corner, I'll be able to see the whole V-Mart. Maybe I can figure out where Mrs K is."

C wrote B next to the tree on the map.

"We'll need weapons." A pointed to C's image of the Sporting Goods store. "Old Man Fletcher keeps a spare key under the trash can around back in the alley."

"How do you know that?" said C.

"I'd rather not say what I do in my private time," said A, avoiding C's questioning gaze.

"Alright," said C as she wrote an A on the Sporting Goods Store.

"I'll go with her," said Annie. C wrote a second A on the store but added a one and two next to them to differentiate them. A was pleased to be A1.

"J and I will sneak into the back of the V-Mart and talk to the demons. See if they'll help us, if they love Mrs K so much," said C. She drew a C and J on the map, adding a heart around them without thinking.

"Let's all meet back at the Carpet King van as soon as we can. They might start the ritual at any second," she said.

They stood up from the booth. Annie grabbed B and pulled him close.

"In case you die," she said and kissed him. He kissed her back, and then they were just making out in front of everyone. A rolled her eyes and looked away.

C looked at B and Annie and impulsively grabbed Jonathan and kissed him. It did not go as she planned. He pulled back in a panic.

"Am I going to *die?*" he asked. The moment of their first kiss broken, C dragged him towards the door.

"Come on," she said.

"Such a dumb hot," whispered A. She waited near B and Annie impatiently. B finally came up for air, gasping. Annie beamed at him.

"That was nice," she said.

"Beat it a sec, toots," A said to Annie, elbowing her playfully but a bit too hard.

"Toots?" said Annie, rubbing her ribs.

"I'm trying new words." Annie took a few steps away from A and B.

"I'm…" she said.

"Shut up," B said, hugging her.

"Yeah," A said, hugging him back.

They didn't need to say anything else. All was forgiven. They let go of each other and A whipped around to face Annie. "Let's go. I want a sword that shoots flames," she said.

23

The Reunion

On MTV, the soundtrack of Killian's life ended as she emerged back into the lot through a cloud of spiraling smoke. Her glove crackled with power. She was covered head to toe in blood and chunks that were pieces of former humans. She wasn't bothered at all. Her mouth tasted like pennies. She walked back to her RV as all around her, V-Mart Goons went about their business like her new look was no big thing. She was pleased to see they had finished making the library accessible. Her glove beeped, and its hum wound down audibly. A small red battery light flashed on the power unit strapped to her arm. All that carnage of magnets and power had drained it. Tiffany appeared at her side, ready with a box of chunky square power cells designed by Vlada.

"Freshen me up," Killian said to her. "I'm also going to need a costume change."

Tiffany popped the used power cell out and tossed it to the ground with practiced ease while they were walking.

"Hail there, fellow occultists," said a voice from behind them. It was Augustus.

Killian didn't stop, but Tiffany did as she looked back over her shoulder and saw what at first she thought was someone dressed in The Count Suckula mascot costume. She had spent time in that thing early in her career at Vass Enterprises, being groped by customers young and old, before Killian had rescued her by bringing her into the inner circle.

"Maybe *I* should speak, brother?" said Giles.

"Nonsense. I'm better with the jammy ones," said Augustus.

Killian stopped realizing Tiffany was not with her. She turned on her heels and saw *it*.

"Hello. What's this?" she asked.

The Count bowed, covering its head hole. Next to it, Chad Baxter waved empathically.

"We are Augustus Alexander Vass the third and…"

"Giles Alexander Vass the fourth…"

"And we are at your service, madam," finished Augustus.

"You're… *them?*" said Killian as Tiffany remembered what she was doing and slotted a new power cell onto the glove. The device whoomped back to life.

"We are indeed *them*. Please ignore our jaunty carapace. It is a mere inconvenience of embodiment we hope to shortly remedy," said Augustus.

"We are in a tonic. Perhaps with your great powers, you could assist us to re-obtain our bodies?" sucked up Giles.

Killian was fascinated by this clearly magical construction and those orbs; she must learn how they held a soul stable and contained. For years, she and Vlada had been working on a product she'd dubbed a *Soul Jar* which would allow her to trap souls, human and otherwise. If she could come into possession of these orbs, Vlada would surely be able to reverse engineer their magic? Vlada had also theorized they could be used as a temporary repository in case of death, before transferring to a new, younger, tighter vessel. This thing proved it was possible. Permanent death was a choice and Killian refused its offer.

Chad Baxter filled the silence of Killian's racing mind.

"I'm Chad Baxter. I work at the Sizzler."

Killian laughed at this teen boy's confidence as she slowly walked towards The Count.

"You are my idiot forebearers who botched the ritual, angered The Great Maw and put our family's plan to rule the world a hundred years behind schedule."

The brothers were shocked that a woman would speak to them like this.

"We had minor trouble with the ritual. Mostly logistical," Augustus explained in his Augustus way.

Giles put it more bluntly: "Augustus sullied our virgin," he said without embellishment.

"A mere misunderstanding on my part. Women have several ritual orifices. I was simply confused in the dark of a closet," Augustus explained, making it worse.

Giles attempted to recover by falling back on decorum.

"You have us at a disadvantage, madam. We do not know your name as you know ours," he said.

Killian was very close to The Count now. She reached out and gently stroked its fangs.

"Call me 'madam' again and I'll drink your whole head," she said softly in a way that made Giles terrified and Augustus tingle.

Giles made The Count take step back.

Augustus couldn't help himself.

"You are quite the…"

Giles made The Count elbow itself to get Augustus to stop talking.

"For once in your life, brother, shut it and let me speak," said Giles in the tone he used on his long dead children, before they were long dead, of course.

Augustus' orb shifted back into The Count's head.

"We have seen your power. We suggest an alliance," said Giles.

Killian laughed with her whole body.

"What could I ever need of you?" she said through a deep snort.

"The ritual is precise and complex. We are the only people to have ever completed it," said Giles.

"And how did that work out for you?"

Giles made the The Count stick out its chest and gestured to its body.

"It is one hundred years later. We walk. We talk, and we *endure*, madam."

"Tiff, get me a big straw," said Killian with a raised eyebrow,

"May we have your name so as to avoid being drunk?" begged Giles.

Killian put out her arms and spun in place.

"I am Killian Alexandra Vass the first… and only."

Augustus' orb rushed back to the face.

"We are *kin*. This ritual. The Great Maw's power. It is all our destiny."

"NO!" screamed Killian. It echoed loudly. All over the lot, V-Mart Goons stopped working and turned to make sure Killian wasn't about to blast them out of their skin.

Killian pointed her Power Glove at The Count.

"It is mine. You will kneel before me, great great great uncles, and I will allow you to serve me or I will destroy your souls."

She lowered her hand to point at the ground.

Giles knelt The Count immediately.

"Brother?" said Augustus for the first time in his life, unsure. A woman had never cowered him until now.

"This is the only way, brother," said Giles.

Killian looked at Chad Baxter, "And you?"

Chad Baxter knelt, too. He raised his eyes to gaze upon this goddess. He was smitten.

"Will you go to prom with me? I'm still Chad Baxter."

24

The Plan

A let herself into the back door of the Dock's Sporting Goods store and threw the key over her shoulder as she entered. It had been exactly where she had said it would be. Annie picked it up and closed the back door. A flipped a switch and the store lit up as rows of florescent lights fired up, illuminating rack after rack of sports equipment, as well as a large cabinet behind the counter filled with firearms and locked up tight. Annie grabbed a shopping cart.

The store PA turned on: "Welcome to Dock's Sporting Goods, a place to create memories," said the man himself in a prerecorded message. "I may not remember my legendary no-no but that doesn't mean you have to forget your children's faces smiling at the joy of hitting a ball with a bat, hitting a free throw, doing whatever it is they do in Ice Hockey or letting rip with an M16. Spend over 300 dollars and get a set of hair curlers free. Limited to one set per customer."

A ran her hand over a locked glass counter case containing handguns.

"I'd like to kill someone," she said, letting an inside thought outside. Annie examined two different hockey sticks, one red and the other blue, trying to discern the difference. They looked identical to her.

"Let's not do killing. Do you think William would like this one?" she asked, holding up the red stick. A shrugged.

"We don't sport as a rule," she said as she eyeballed an archery set. She looked at Annie and took a moment to formulate a question that wouldn't insult Annie but would get to the point of her concerns.

"What are your intentions with him?"

Annie put the red hockey stick in the cart and pushed it to the next section. A kept pace with her.

"Right now? Hand stuff I guess, but like long term…" she trailed off, gathering her thoughts.

Annie noticed that A was staring intently at her. She obviously wanted a real answer. Annie wondered if A had feelings for B. A didn't. It was cliche, but she really thought of B as a brother. They had once played doctor a million years ago, but it had been super weird. Being honest with herself, A wasn't sure she was as into boys as she was into girls. She'd had some *experiences* that had got her thinking and feeling unsure about that kind of thing.

"I like him. He's sweet. Most of the boys who want to date me treat me like a prize. I get it. B doesn't make me feel like my job is being popular," said Annie half quoting *Heathers* to make her point. Annie watched A thinking.

"Okay. That makes sense. You can stay for now," A said, and just like that, even if she didn't know it yet, A had accepted Annie as one of them.

"Next… wounds?" A said as she slid open a glass cabinet that held hunting knives, machetes, hand axes and hatchets.

"Are we maiming or hacking like with a hatchet? Ooh, hatchet is a fun word. Hatchet. Hatchet. Say it."

Annie compared a wooden and an aluminum baseball bat.

"Hatchet. It *is* fun, but how about a light bonking on the head to knock someone out instead? Less mess. Less *world* to get on you," reasoned Annie.

A took the wooden bat. She swung it wildly a few times.

"I like your thinking, hot girl. Wood could break a jaw, I guess. Snapping. Snapping. Snap," she said. A put the wooden bat in the cart with a nod.

"I'm taking a crossbow as well. Just for fun. And nunchucks. For chucking," said A as she walked off.

B crept through the Carpet King lot. Making it across the intersection unseen had been easy, given the amount of destruction. He had quickly moved from vehicle to vehicle. Avoiding stepping in what used to be people. Not that they looked much like people anymore. Except for the skeletons. B told his brain they were just Halloween decorations, so he didn't have to think about what had just happened to them. The smell was the worst part. It made him gag the whole way. B would never eat bacon again.

Halfway across the lot, B tripped where he always tripped and for the first time after tripping on whatever this was for maybe the hundredth time, he decided to investigate.

He ran his hand through the long grass and found it. It was metal and cold and was stuck in the ground hard. He pulled, but it wouldn't budge. He was about to put his whole weight behind it when a slashing light cut through the dark of the lot.

B ducked and lay prone in the grass as the light passed through the air he had just been standing in. Once it was gone, B lifted his head. A V-Mart Goon in an open top jeep with a mounted spotlight was parked next to the tree on the sidewalk on the other side of the fence. B had come in through the Main Street side of the lot, if he had come down Woodhill, he would have walked right into this guy. There was no way to get up the tree without being spotted.

"We are boned," he said quietly to himself.

In the back alley behind the V-Mart was a short brick wall that blocked off the back of the lot to the woods and the creek behind it. Against the wall stood three rusted bins for the V-Mart. C and Jonathan now crouched behind them, hiding as two V-Mart Goons carrying flashlights patrolled the perimeter of the store.

C and Jonathan had gone all the way down the last block of Main Street to cut through the woods. They had crossed along the big pipe over the creek to get behind the store without being seen. C had held Jonathan's hand the whole way. While he'd never been on the pipe, C knew it well.

Just before they reached the back door these two assholes had announced themselves by talking loudly. One Goon was recounting the plot of a recent episode of *Baywatch*, where Billy Warlock as Eddie Kramer had dreams about a ghost in a lighthouse. Goon Two had a high nasal laugh that echoed through the night as they moved off around the far corner. Jonathan didn't get why they were making fun of that episode. It had scared the hell out of him.

Once C was sure they weren't coming back, she and Jonathon moved fast to the rear door of the store. Jonathan fumbled with his keys in a way that made C nervous. Finally, he got the key in the lock, and they quickly opened the door and entered the store.

They were soon standing in the last aisle, listening. MTV was still playing, but someone had turned the volume down after a Milli Vanilli song had come on. C couldn't help herself. She had to see what was happening on the lot, so she crawled to the windows and peered out.

The lightning lady was exiting her sick RV in a hot pink power suit that gave off Jackie O vibes. She walked across the lot like she owned it and descended some scaffold stairs into the giant ass hole they had ripped open. The lady was followed by a prissy looking young woman, The Goddamn Count and Goddamn Chad Baxter.

"Goddamn old dudes," she said. Jonathan had joined her at the window tentatively.

"Oh man. Look what they've done," he said.

C couldn't believe it either. They had sat on that curb night after night after night, never knowing there was secret occult library vault complete with altar thing right beneath their feet. No one had known, she supposed, except these Vassholes. Oh, and Jonathan who read plaques when he was cleaning.

"It'll be okay. We can make them rebuild the car park," she said to Jonathan, placing a hand on his arm.

"No, my car!" he said, pointing. Some V-Mart Goons had left three Monster Big Sucks melting on the hood. "The condensation could ruin the clear coat," he said, like it was a huge deal. C had no response to that one. She moved, staying low, heading towards the front counter and the office behind it. Jonathan followed. She went to open the door, but Jonathon reached out and took her hand, looking her right in the eye.

"Before we go in, I have to tell you something important," he said, suddenly as serious as hell.

"Okay," said C, unsure where this was going and hoping he wasn't about to 'L' word her…

"I lied to you before."

"You did?"

Great. Not the L word she was scared of. Phew.

"Yeah, and I'm sorry."

"Okay."

Jonathan took a deep breath.

"There are no mean cats," he admitted.

"Right?" C wasn't getting why this was so important.

"It was the Do-Beccy things. The demons. I didn't want you to figure it out when you met them and then hate me for not telling you. I like you. A lot. I think I lo… "

WHOA. WHOA. WHOA. *It was happening.*

C cut him off with a kiss. It was the only thing she could think of. She pulled back.

"Cool, I appreciate your honesty," she said with two hands on his shoulders. Goddamn, he *is* hot, she thought.

"I appreciate that you're banging. Can we make out again?" he asked with horny teen boy energy.

"Yeah, later. The demons?"

"Oh, yeah." He gave her the goofiest of smiles and she melted. Jonathan was nothing like she'd expected, and that had been jarring, but she'd realized he was sweet so that was nice.

"Ah, be careful. They're super scary," he said as he reached up and twisted the doorknob. The door swung open to reveal The Teeth.

They were lying in a pile like sleeping kittens, bored and dozing. C thought they were *adorable.* They paid no mind to Jonathan and C as they entered.

"They *do* look like cats. Ask them if they'll help us save your

Mom," said C.

Head Teeth opened one eye and then sat up, using its paws to rub the sleep out of its eyes. Gap Teeth burped, pulled a piece of bat wing out of its teeth and started chewing on it.

"How?" asked Jonathan, looking confused.

"Speak Korean to them," said C.

"Oh, I don't speak Korean. It's way too hard."

C almost fell over.

"Did you think I did?"

He figured it out.

"Oh no!"

"Dude!"

Thank God he was *sweet*, C thought.

25

The Ritual

Below street level in the Vass manor library, everything was ready to begin the ritual. The altar and its symbols sparkled, returned to their former glory through elbow grease and copious amounts of Turtle Wax.

Killian stood before the altar. Tiffany was to her left, The Count was to her right. Chad Baxter loitered awkwardly outside the arcane circle. He figured if standing on a crack broke your mamma's back it was best not to stand on whatever this weird *Dungeons and Dragons* nerd shit was. Three specially selected Occultists stood nearby, ready to assist.

On the rim above them were gathered the rest of the Occultists, as well as Killian's team of Scientists, Technicians and general Goons. Some were still working at computers or monitoring CRT screens. Other having finished their tasks were there to witness history being made. More than a few sucked on Big Sucks. Jackhammer Guy and his boys had pushed to the front, displacing some nerdy, and now somewhat bitter, Technicians.

Killian placed the *Invocatio Dentium* on a metal bookstand

to her right. She opened it to a page she'd marked with a *Strawberry Shortcake* bookmark. The book was filled with layers of text, the original Latin ritual written by quill in blood, although since overwritten many times in many languages and then annotated in red pen with notes, questions and commentary. Fastened with a paperclip to the page by Vlada was a small cheat sheet of the ritual in English. In her beautiful modified cursive it outlined each step. Printed on the opposite page was a smudged woodcut print of The Great Maw in all its terror and glory. Killian stroked the print with her Power Gloved hand and then looked up at her people.

"Are we ready?" she asked.

A Scientist Goon looked up from her monitor. On the CRT screen, the red and green pixel circles overlapped and pulsed in time with each other, now perfectly in sync.

"Space and time are aligned and dilated. We are go," said the Science Goon loud enough for all to hear.

Killian pumped her ungloved fist.

"Let's fucking go. Let's rule the world!" she said. The Goons all roared in approval.

An Occultist rolled a steel cart into position on Killian's left. On it, everything she needed for the ritual was laid out in order.

"This is really happening," thought Killian. "I'm standing at the altar about to say the words." She didn't need Vlada's cheat sheet. She knew it by her cold black twisted heart.

She spoke loudly in Latin with all the power and projection of an overconfident drama camp kid.

"We of the earth."

The Occultist next to Killian picked up a large salt rock to hand to her but The Count stepped forward and put his hand on the rock.

"May we?" Giles asked.

"We love this part," said Augustus.

Killian nodded and the Occultist gave the rock to The Count, who in turn passed it to Killian.

Killian licked the rock with her long tongue. She placed it on a corner of the altar. On the marble floor beneath their feet the occult symbol for earth began to glow with energy that spread through the connected golden tendrils inlaid in the floor towards the altar.

"We of the divine *feminine*," Killian continued in Latin.

The Count handed her a silver chalice of red wine. She drank from it and then spit wine onto the altar before placing it down opposite the salt rock.

The wine sizzled and evaporated in scarlet steam. On the floor the symbol for female power glowed and spread its power towards the altar.

"We of the powerful *masculine*," said Killian, rolling her eyes at this part.

The Count picked up the high tech replica of the ritual dagger. Both Giles and Augustus were impressed and took their time admiring it. Annoyed they weren't moving quickly enough, Killian pulled the dagger away from them with the magnets of her glove and dipped it into the silver chalice.

The male symbol now also glowed with power which started to flow through the tendrils. The glowing symbols entwined upwards, nearly reaching the center of the altar. Each element, each gift, was a key in a cosmic lock.

"This is making me *horny*," Chad Baxter said, too loudly. Tiffany elbowed him to shut up.

"We who stole fire from the gods," said Killian.

The Count handed her a black candle and matches. With a

flourish, Killian struck the wax match off the altar. She used it to light the candle. She put the candle down and held her left hand over its flame until it blackened the skin of her palm. The pain was intense, but she barely felt it, having practiced the ritual burn many times over the years, learning to shut down the pain centers of her brain and endure. The fourth symbol glowed brightly.

"We that breathe deep the air," she said.

She put her hand out, waiting. The Count looked at the cart in confusion.

"Ah… Gus?" said Giles.

"Hmm," said Augustus as his orb scanned the cart. An annoyed Occultist stepped over and pointed at an object neither of them recognized.

"I was about to say it was that," said Augustus petulantly. The Count handed Killian a portable fan. Killian had made some modern adjustments to the ritual, after all, who owned a bellows anymore? She placed the fan on the altar and turned it on. A strong gust of magical wind and swirling dust from the bookshelves rushed into the air. Five symbols now throbbed and glowed, each feeding their energy into each other and towards the altar.

"We who came from water," said Killian.

The Occultist was ready this time. They handed the next item to The Count, who in turn passed it to Killian. She twisted open the bottle of lightly sparkling mineral water and splashed it on the altar. It hissed and steamed, and the sixth symbol began to glow.

B waited for the others next to the Carpet King van, bracing himself against the wind. It whipped the long grass into spirals.

It was loud enough that he didn't hear C and Jonathan coming. B jumped out of his skin when he saw Jonathan, not realizing who it was and punched him in the face. Jonathan didn't react. B felt like he'd hit a brick wall.

"Damn," B said rubbing his fist. "Sorry about your face."

Jonathan shrugged it off. "Sorry about your *hand*," he said.

"We had to go halfway down Woodhill and over the creek to get past a jeep," said C as Annie and A emerged from the dark near the laundry wall with a shopping cart. They struggled to push it through the grass. Jonathan went over and helped.

"We're alive and have weapons!" said Annie, with her usual cheeriness.

"I got nunchucks and a crossbow," said A, almost twinning her tone. A swung her nunchucks in demonstration and Annie lent back deftly out of the way to avoid being hit, like she had already had to do this a few times.

Everyone armed up. C took the crossbow from a reluctant A. B grabbed the red hockey stick which made Annie's heart soar. Annie took the wooden bat and Jonathan grabbed the aluminum one.

"Did you find Mrs K?" asked C.

B shook his head. "I couldn't even get up the tree. There is a V-Mart dude with a big light in a jeep right there."

"Do we have demon friends?" asked A.

"No," said C, not elaborating.

"I don't speak Korean," said Jonathan, with great shame.

Annie perked up, "Oh, I speak Korean."

They all looked at her.

"You do?" asked C.

"Totally not fluently, but my first and third nannies were Korean. I can muddle through," said Annie.

"That is so cool," said B, looking at her in awe. The awe was shared by A.

"This day has flipped my whole understanding of the universe on its head," she said.

Thunder rumbled in the sky above them.

"It sounds like the Vassholes have started the ritual. I don't think we have long," said C.

"The V-Mart's empty. We can use the CCTV to look for Mrs K while Annie talks to the demons," said C.

"Wait," said B. "I stashed some fireworks in the van so my Dad wouldn't find them. Maybe we can use them," He grabbed the van door and pulled it open.

Inside the van, someone screamed.

Killian took the dagger out the chalice and raised it up to her heart.

"We who offer purity and blood,' she said in Latin.

Giles and Augustus' orbs inside the The Count swung around, looking.

"Whom of your human chattel is the virgin?' said Giles.

Killian looked at The Count and then towards Tiffany.

"Where the fuck is my virgin?" Killian was so in the zone she spoke in Latin.

Tiffany didn't understand and shook her head, looking puzzled.

"WHERE IS FUCKING GINA?" Killian yelled at her in English.

Gina screamed from inside the Carpet King van. B screamed from outside the Carpet King van. Gina stopped when she saw it was just some kids.

"Oh my God. Sorry. I thought they'd found me," she said.

"Who are you?" asked C.

"I'm Gina. I work for Miss Vass."

C grabbed Gina with both hands and pulled her out of the van, lifting her off her feet.

"Where is our Mrs K?" she said, right in Gina's face.

"The store owner? I can show you. Please don't hurt me." Gina cowered.

"Do you know how we can stop the ritual?" asked B.

"I've already stopped it. I was meant to be sacrificed. I don't want to die a virgin, *or* an intern," cried Gina. C set her down on the ground.

"Talk fast or I'll let my friend here nunchuck you," said C.

A swung her nunchucks for effect and almost whacked herself in the face.

"I'm the bad witch," she said.

"So bad," said Annie.

"Thanks babes," said A and they high-fived.

"You *agreed* to be sacrificed?" C asked Gina.

"Miss Vass promised me a full time position and said that once she had The Maw's power she'd return me to this realm. The Maw devours bodies but their souls live in its hell realm as a part of its collection," she explained with a shrug.

"Like the old dudes," said B.

"The orbs in the misogynist cup thing, yes. You have to believe me, I'm on your side. I just want to live," said Gina.

The kids huddled.

"I think we should trust her," said B.

"You don't have a clean record in that department," said C.

"I just like to help people," B said.

"No one admits to being a virgin unless they really are," said

Annie.

"Maybe…" said C.

A broke from the huddle and turned back to Gina.

"If you're not a virgin I'll tape all your holes shut and force you to drink a New Coke and then slam a whole packet of Mentos."

She mimed an explosion from all of her orifices in alphabetical order.

"We call it the fresh maker," C added.

"I swear on my life I'm virgin and I will help you," said Gina horrified.

"Maybe we can just run out the clock? Like a sport. That's a thing, right? No virgin. No Maw?" said B.

"We still need to get Mrs K. We don't know what they are going to do to her," said C.

26

Where in the world is Mrs K?

In an undisclosed location not far away, Mrs K was handcuffed to a metal bench. She was working on freeing herself. On the ground in front of her were the bodies of three V-Mart Goons, beaten to a pulp.

27

Secret Hand Stuff

Killian slammed the dagger down on the altar.

"I knew it! I knew that size zero bitch would betray me. Find her! She can't have gotten far in those heels," she yelled to no one and everyone. Tiffany gave the order to start the search for Gina. Around the lot, Goons rolled out in their jeeps, each with a driver and searchlight operator.

"Now, is anyone here a virgin?" asked Killian. Her gathered Goons all voiced 'no' in various flavors. Killian snorted in disbelief.

"None of you science nerds have V cards?!" she asked, staring directly at the monitoring station team. Several Scientists suddenly became incredibly busy with things they totally needed to do right now.

"We have a lot of after-hours orgies," someone unseen yelled out.

"Okay. Gross," said Killian. She turned to Tiffany and looked her up and down.

"Tiff?"

Tiffany had been prepared for this moment but panicked

and blurted out, "I do mouth stuff. A *lot* of mouth stuff." Killian was dubious.

"Does mouth stuff count?" she asked everyone. Her Goons answered like a chorus with each member singing a slightly different tune.

"I shouldn't think so," said Augustus.

"Oh, it counts," said Giles.

"Okay, what if Tiff *pretends* to be a virgin? I mean, will The Maw really know?" Killian asked.

Giles made the The Count gesture dramatically, indicating its current situation.

"Oh, it will *know*," said Augustus.

"We are living testament to the fact that the consequences are rather unpleasant," said Giles.

"Living *dead* testament," Augustus clarified.

Killian groaned with the energy of a teenager shouting at her parents that this wasn't fair. It *wasn't* fair.

"Ten years' worth of planning, and no one suggested we should have a backup virgin? One of you better find Gina, or I'm going to lightning all of you and move to Tahiti," Killian said, sitting down on the altar sulkily.

No one noticed Gina and C peering over the self-serve ice freezer near the corner of the V-Mart. The others were hiding down the side of the store.

"Your Mrs K is in that truck," said Gina, pointing at a V-Mart box truck near a semi-trailer.

"That's good. We can use the semi for cover," said C.

C and Gina ducked back around the corner to join the others.

"Everyone good with the new plan?" asked C. Everyone nodded silently. C wanted to make sure they all understood their roles.

"You're sure you can talk to the demons?" she asked Annie, who nodded vigorously.

"I think soap," said Annie in Korean. They all looked at Jonathan for confirmation.

"It *sounds* like when Mom yells at me," he said.

"We have to hurry. It'll all be for nothing if she finds another virgin," stressed Gina.

Annie gasped loudly as something occurred to her.

"Oh no. Chad Baxter."

C's eyes went wide.

"Chad Baxter," she said.

"Chad Baxter," said B with an 'oh shit' tone.

"Chaaaad Baaaaxter," said A, sounding out every letter like a total weirdo.

"Chad Baxter?" said C, not getting it.

A avoided all eye contact.

"Chad Baxter," repeated A in a tone indicating that she might have verified knowledge that Chad Baxter was *not* in fact a virgin.

It took a full three seconds for C's brain to figure out how A was aware of Chad Baxter's boned or un-boned status. C blinked hard in shock.

"CHAD BAXTER??!!"

A glared at everyone, daring them to challenge her choices.

"I told you no one was to ask about my private time in the sporting goods store," she said.

"Chad Baxter," said Annie in a positive *You Go, Girl* way.

"I don't get it," said Jonathan.

B got it, a full ten seconds after C.

"No. Chad Baxter?" he said.

A punched him hard in the arm.

"Yes. Chad Baxter," she said.

"Chad Baxter..." B considered.

"Chad Baxter," said A, meaning 'fuck off'.

Gina had no idea what was happening.

"Whoever this Chad Baxter is doesn't matter. Killian will find *someone*. We have to get the dagger away from her," Gina said, desperate to get them back on track.

"But we don't stand a chance against her lightning glove thing," said Annie.

"It's powerful, but it chews through batteries real fast if she uses the magnets at a high setting for too long," said Gina.

"Hold up, I just figured something out," said B, suddenly running into the dark towards the Carpet King lot.

"Chad Baxter?" said C softly, so A knew it wasn't judgment. She just wanted to understand. A had never ever said anything about liking a guy. C had even wondered if she was into girls. C thought her mutual drooling over Jonathan might have been a cover.

"Shut up,' said A.

She looked at C.

"Alright, but I mean, Chad Baxter," C said.

"Chad Baxter. It's not... we're not... we just.... Chad Baxter has strong hands," she explained. "And I get lonely."

"Chad Baxter," said C in a tone that showed she was reconsidering her judgment.

C really couldn't talk. She had lost her virginity only last year to a bass player for a shitty punk band that she hadn't even heard play and couldn't remember the name of. It'd happened one lonely Saturday night after they'd run out of gas and coasted their van into the V-Mart lot. Mrs K had let them fill up for free. Tall, dark and handsome, the bass player had swaggered up to C sitting on the curb, and asked if she knew where he could score some dope. She, like a dope, had taken him to the Carpet King to sell him one of B's joints. She had made the first move and before she knew it, it had happened and was over. She had no regrets but she'd decided to not exactly advertise that it'd happened, either.

B returned out of the dark, holding a dirt encrusted ritual dagger.

"Is this something important?" he asked. Gina snatched it away from him.

"Holy shit. This is the *original* ritual dagger. Where'd you find it?" she asked.

C grabbed the dagger back from Gina and returned it to B. She didn't want Gina holding on to it, just in case.

"I've been tripping over it for years," he said.

The original dagger had never been reclaimed from the gardens of Vass Manor after that Halloween night a hundred years ago. It had sat half-buried until it was completely buried as the town of Underwood expanded onto the grounds of the former Vass estate. It had been churned up when the charred remains of the burnt down building on the now empty lot had been demolished long before the weirds were out of Pampers and had sat, once more half-buried in the overgrown grass for season after season, unnoticed except for a kid who tripped over it every time he made his way to the Carpet King van.

"Is it important?" C asked Gina.

"It's useless, just crazy that you found it. You could use a plastic spork and The Maw would still grant you the gift - most of the ritual is just nonsense. The key is the virgin blood," explained Gina, much to their disappointment.

"It doesn't matter, we don't want whatever its gift is," said C.

"Yeah, you kind of do. The Maw grants the power to shape the world," said Gina.

There was still a part of her that was a true believer, even if she didn't want to die for that belief.

"That's a pretty *vague* power," said B.

Gina was pissed they weren't getting it.

"It basically means you can-" Gina didn't have time to finish.

They had been found. A V-Mart jeep had stopped in front of them. A Goon was pointing his searchlight right at them.

"Shit! Go! Everyone stick to the plan," yelled C as they all ran off in different directions.

A and Annie bolted into the alley at the back of the V-Mart.

C and Jonathan ran onto Woodhill street and towards the box truck that held Mrs K.

Gina froze. B went to run off, too, but couldn't leave her. He dropped his hockey stick and swung his backpack around so it was on his chest. He pulled out a large Roman Candle, bit the fuse short with his teeth and lit it with a plastic V-Mart lighter.

The V-Mart Goon operating the spotlight vaulted out to grab Gina.

KABOOM!

The fireworks rocketed out of the tube like a fire hose of sparks and hit the Goon directly in the chest, also showering Gina and B in colorful sparks and smoke and stuff. The Goon screamed. His cheap nylon V-Mart boiler suit was on fire. He stopped, dropped and rolled as he tried to put himself out. B lifted the candle and it kept firing into the sky for a few seconds. Gina picked up B's hockey stick and whacked the Goon for good measure. The driver Goon fled into the lot as B dropped the empty tube and pulled out another firework.

He had twenty, nineteen now, Roman Candles of various sizes plus twelve rockets, six cherry bombs and a handful of other throwable bangers he'd made himself from gunpowder stolen from his father's shotgun shells, plastic tubing and electrical tape. Finally, his love of fire was paying off.

Gina jumped into the driver's seat of the jeep and took off her heels.

"Come on!" she yelled. B jumped in the jeep as Gina ground the transmission into first gear. They peeled out, bumping over both the curb and the unconscious Goon and drove past the semi-trailer. When they reached the intersection Gina swerved erratically left and right to avoid the debris of Killian's cop-apocalypse. A cop-alypse? Behind them, three V-Mart jeeps now gave chase. The jeep lurched and made a mechanical crunching sound every time Gina changed gears.

"Can you drive stick?" she asked B.

"I play a lot of *OutRun*," B offered.

"Just great," said Gina as she pointed the jeep towards Main Street and floored it.

B climbed into the back and stood up, bracing on the steel piping the spotlight was mounted on. He lit another candle and aimed it at the closest pursuing jeep.

The firework screamed as it fired again and again in a straight line and exploded in sparks when it hit the windscreen. The driver threw his hands up, but was too late to protect himself from being shotgunned with broken windscreen glass. The jeep clipped a wrecked cop car and rolled over like something out of the movies. The spotlight Goon was thrown clear but hurt when he bounced off another wrecked vehicle. The second jeep swerved to avoid the first jeep but it was too late. It hit the overturned jeep and sent it spinning across the street like a top. The second jeep's engine died in a splutter. The driver's nose was broken from slamming into the steering wheel. The spotlight operator was nursing broken ribs from where his chest had hit the metal piping. Only the third jeep remained operable as it drifted past the other two through a plume of smoke from a still burning cop car.

B turned back to Gina to celebrate and saw that they were clear of the intersection. They were already a block up Main Street heading away from the V-Mart. Gina was making a run for it.

"Hey, turn back," said B over the noise of the engine.

"Are you crazy!? She's going to blast us off the planet!" said Gina, grinding up another gear.

"You said you'd help," bargained B. "It's better she blasts us than finishes the ritual."

Gina groaned but turned the wheel hard. The jeep spun around and turned back down Main Street and towards the V-Mart.

This was the last thing the Goon in final jeep was expecting. The virgin and the punk kid were now driving right at him. He swerved and bounced onto the sidewalk in front of the liquor store. He hit the brakes hard to stop the jeep from smashing into the front of the store, unintentionally almost squashing two teen jocks in letterman jackets who were walking past.

28

The Storm

Thunder boomed, and rain began to fall in swirling torrents as Killian rose from the pit in fury, wet but still fabulous. She looked past her Goons and the V-Mart vehicles just as B and Gina reentered the intersection.

B fired a rocket vaguely in her direction. He wanted her attention, and he got it as the firework hit a nearby van and rained sparks on her head.

The Count and Chad Baxter, standing behind her a couple of steps down, ducked.

Killian did not.

"Who is that?" Killian asked as the jeep weaved around the destroyed vehicles in the intersection.

"Ah… there are several pesky street urchins floating about. Pay them no mind, they are harmless," said Augustus.

"Although they *do* seem to have acquired your virgin," said Giles.

Killian squinted. She really should have been wearing her glasses, and her smoky eye shadow was melting down her face, making her look a little crazed.

"GINA! YOU *GOONIE!*" she screamed.

Killian raised her Power Glove and closed it into a fist. A burst of lightning whipped down from the storm and into the glove.

In the back of a V-Mart box truck Mrs K was rubbing her wrists together. It had taken her longer than expected to get loose of the cuffs. Her left thumb was sore where she'd dislocated it to slide free. It was now back where it belonged, and that was all that mattered. She was concerned about the racket she'd been hearing outside the truck for the last ten minutes. She needed to make sure her kids were safe. She stepped over the downed Goons to the roller door at the back of the truck. She opened it with one strong tug to find the shocked faces of Courtney and Jonathan looking at her.

"Where is that fancy V-Mart *amkae* (bitch) and what has she done to my store?" she asked.

C pointed and Mrs K followed her finger just in time to see Killian unleash a bolt of lightning at B and Gina's jeep as it passed the front of the Sizzler. It missed. The store's front windows exploded, *Highlander* quickening style, in a wave from left to right, that seemed to be chasing after the jeep.

"Into the store now. Go!" Mrs K yelled as she jumped down from the truck. They all started running.

Gina stopped the jeep behind the Sizzler. She and B were both shaken and covered in broken glass. They brushed as much off themselves as they could and checked to see if they were hurt. They both had angry red scratches all over, but there was nothing major.

"I told you she'd blast us," said Gina.

Their hair had frizzed up from the static of the lightning. No matter where he looked, B could still see the afterglow of a white line across his vision. B had already seen what the Vass woman could do when they were inside the Sizzler, but feeling the blast miss him by inches had terrified him. Still, he had to do whatever he could to keep his friends safe, and that meant distracting this woman.

"Where am I going?" asked Gina.

B pulled out three of his biggest candles and shortened the fuses again with his teeth.

"Circle back around and get closer to her this time. We have to keep her firing at us so she wastes her battery."

"You're crazy," said Gina. Behind them, the final Goon jeep roared around the corner towards them.

B lit a candle as Gina gripped the gear shift and kicked the jeep back into motion.

B's aim was thrown off. The fireworks whizzed out of the tube and missed the jeep in a wide arc. They skipped along the ground before exploding in white hot sparks. B was pissed with himself. He'd wasted one of the big ones. He reached into his backpack as he held on for dear life with his other hand. He pulled out one of his homemade bangers, lit it and tossed it into the path of the pursuing jeep. It blew up with a ear splitting pop under the chasing vehicle. Black smoke billowed from under the jeep. B had hoped it would break something down there, but it kept kept coming after them as they sped around the Sizzler and back into the car park.

From the top of the scaffold stairs, The Count watched Killian as she reloaded her glove, calling down more lightning and walking calmly into the intersection.

Giles swam his red glowing soul orb to the back of The Count's head.

"Augustus, look," he said. Augustus' blue soul orb joined his brother, bumping into him.

"Oh my, brother," he said.

No one was in the library pit. *Their* altar stood alone, still glowing with dark magical energy. Both orbs swung back around, and The Count grabbed Chad Baxter's hand, leading him back down the stairs towards their, and his, mutual destinies.

Killian fired another lightning bolt at the jeep as it sped out of the Sizzler car park and back into the intersection. She struck a power pole, which split and exploded in splinters. Cables snapped and whipped wildly like they were alive all around the intersection. They sparked in arcs of electricity as they touched wrecked cars and the wet tarmac of the road. Gina, against her better judgment, drove the jeep even closer to Killian.

B fired a rocket. It screamed towards her. Quickly, she reached out with the force of her magnets and pulled a nearby manhole cover up to use as a shield. The rocket struck it and exploded, leaving her unharmed.

Killian flung the manhole cover at the retreating jeep. It flipped end over end like a spinning dime and smashed through the front windows of the sporting goods store.

The front door of the V-Mart dinged open as C, Jonathan and Mrs K entered and met Annie and A, coming out.

"Eat their faces with soap!" yelled Annie in Korean.

Leaping past her came The Teeth in all their tiny rage. Johnathon raised his hands to stop them, but they bounded past him.

"Don't let them get wet!" he yelled. His mother gave him a withering look and slapped the back of his head before hugging him.

Head Teeth went straight for the jugular of a V-Mart Scientist operating a console. It tore and ripped out a plug of neck skin and blood spurted in pulses like a fountain. The Scientist fell straight backwards like a felled tree, eyes rolling into the back of his head as he turned white from blood loss. Head Teeth rode him down to the ground in joy, looking back lovingly at Mrs K and waving a tiny paw.

Gina made yet another pass at Killian, who was standing in the center of the intersection waiting, daring them to approach with her glove charged with lightning.

B shot his last big candle at her.

Killian opened her fist and fired lightning back.

The lightning intercepted the fireworks just three feet from her. She was hit with firework debris and engulfed in a burst of sparks and colors.

"HIT!" yelled B, looking back to see how hit she actually was.

"Great. If you singed her outfit, she's going to be pissed," said Gina.

The sparks cleared, and Killian was, in fact, both singed *and* pissed. She turned the power dial on her control unit to eleven, and the glove hummed loudly. Rain turned to steam as it hit the glove and tiny forks of lightning crackled all over it. Killian had already killed a lot of people today, but Gina and this Goddamn punk kid she was going to fucking obliterate.

Killian was completely unaware that the V-Mart lot behind her had become a battle zone. A, C, Annie, Jonathan and Mrs K defended the front doors of the V-Mart with their assorted weaponry as the chaos of The Teeth unfolded in front of them.

Vass Enterprises employees were running all over the lot. Some fought back. Many abandoned their posts. A brave, or possibly stupid, few stuck to the plan and tried to keep working.

Cyclops Teeth grinned at Jackhammer Guy, who had been standing against Killian's RV, sipping coffee. He screamed in a very un-Jackhammer Guy way at the tiny monster and threw his coffee at it. He tried to backpedal but slipped and fell onto the wet ground. Cyclops Teeth went straight for his exposed right nipple and ripped it off with a roar.

Spider Teeth climbed into the robes of a V-Mart Occultist who grabbed at her body, trying to stop it.

"HELP! HELP!" she screamed to a boiler suited Goon standing near her with a cattle prod. The Goon, in panic, tried to hit Spider Teeth but instead jabbed the Occultist. The woman fell to the ground, flailing and twitching. Spider Teeth emerged from the neck hole of the Occultist's robe. It used its strong paws to force her mouth open and tore a paw-full of teeth straight out of her mouth and ate them. The sickening sound of teeth crunching on teeth was the last thing the Occultist heard.

The Goon with the prod dropped it in fear and turned to run. Mrs K whacked him across the face with her baseball bat with the grace and enthusiasm of a Little Leaguer; it was lacking form but effective as hell. The Goon crumpled to the ground, probably not dead but maybe dead. Mrs K didn't care. She swapped her bat for the abandoned cattle prod with a satisfied smile.

A few feet away, A was swinging her nunchucks at anyone trying to take shelter in the store. One panicked Scientist got too close and she hit him hard on the arms. There was a deep crack on his left forearm. He turned and ran away.

"Happy Halloween," A called after him. She was having a great time.

In the library pit, The Count picked up the high tech ritual dagger from where Killian had left it on the altar. So far, no one had noticed them.

"Giles," said Augustus in a rare shared moment of brotherly affection.

"Yes, brother, yes. All that power," said Giles in reverence.

"Ours."

"As it should be."

"Now it is time for *US* not to be nice, brother," said Augustus with villainous definitively non-Dalton like malice.

There was one Goon who had been in the V-Mart employee bathroom when Annie had unleashed The Teeth. He had no idea what was happening and picked up the TV remote from the store counter and turned up the volume as the music video for *Epic* by Faith No More started on MTV. He wandered over to the adult section of the magazine aisle and came across Horn Teeth sitting on a shelf again flipping through the Pamela Anderson *Playboy*. Lucky for the Goon, this thing was more interested in the magazine than him. It gave the guy a nod and went back to 'reading' an article. The Goon backed away and left via the back door of the store. He'd hated this job anyway.

Now totally nipple-less, Jackhammer Guy managed to get back on his feet, holding on for dear life to Cyclops Teeth. He threw this thing as hard as he could, halfway across the lot, and it bounced to the feet of Jonathan and C near the front doors.

Jackhammer Guy spotted them, pointed and screamed as he ran around the pit towards them.

"He looks angry with us, but *we* didn't take his nipples," said Jonathan.

Cyclops Teeth scampered towards Mrs K with a nipple still in its teeth, unbothered. It jumped into her waiting arms, cuddling into her.

C raised her crossbow at Jackhammer Guy as he closed the distance to maybe twenty feet away. She thought it might make him stop, but it didn't. She pulled the trigger. The bolt left the bow with a sharp twang. It missed wide and embedded in the hard plastic case of a computer monitor behind him. Jackhammer Guy didn't even flinch as it zipped past his head. He kept running right at them, bleeding from the holes where his nipples used to be.

C turned to A. "Reload."

A and Annie looked at each other.

"We only took one arrow thingy," said A.

"What?" asked C, incredulous. Jackhammer Guy was now only a dozen feet away.

"Run and get it back?" suggested A totally without irony.

Annie took it as intended.

"I'll get it," she said as she ran, taking a wide line to avoid Jackhammer Guy, who was singularly focused on C.

Below them in the pit, The Count stood in front of the altar.

"Chad Baxter. Come lie down for a second," said Augustus. Chad Baxter took a step forward, but then paused. Some primal part of him knew they meant him harm. He started to run, but The Count swiftly kicked Chad Baxter in the shins with his plastic Dracula leg. It hurt bad, and Chad Baxter fell to his knees. He regretted teaching them Karate. The Count grabbed him by the throat and dragged him to the altar. Chad Baxter remembered he'd forgotten to clock out of the Sizzler. He knew now that he never would. Would the

Sizzler Corporation of America pay his outstanding wages to his parents, or would they use some employee punch card-related legal loophole to screw them out of the seventy-five dollars eighty cents he was owed?

Above Chad Baxter, near the front doors of the store, Jonathan wrestled with Cyclops Teeth over the nipple in its mouth as it clung to Mrs K. They tugged back and forth as Cyclops Teeth growled like a dog. Jonathan's biceps won, and he got it away from the creature.

He threw the half-chewed chunk of meat towards Jackhammer Guy, who stopped running as what was left of his right nipple bounced off his chest. He looked down at it and then up at Jonathan.

"Did you just try to give that man back his nipple?" said A.

"It's *his* nipple," said Jonathan.

Jackhammer Guy bent at the waist to pick up his nipple, unsure which side of his chest it came from, as Annie ran back holding the crossbow bolt above her head in victory. She stabbed Jackhammer Guy in the back with it.

"Stabbing!" yelled A, joyously.

Jackhammer Guy grunted in pain and turned towards Annie, holding his nipple in one hand and trying to extract the crossbow bolt with the other.

"Sorry," said Annie.

Jackhammer Guy growled and lunged at her. Annie screamed.

A smacked the shit out Jackhammer Guy's face with her nunchucks. Jackhammer Guy fell down as C, joining them, swung the crossbow across the back of his head and knocked him out cold.

"See, worked like a charm," said A as they all took a breath.

Near a noisy diesel generator, Gap Teeth bit into a thick rubber-enclosed power cable. It jolted with electricity as its teeth hit the copper wire. The generator overloaded and spluttered and across the lot, the work lights started flickering on and off. The surge hit a computer terminal, and it exploded into a Tech Goon's face, blasting him into the side of a van. He slumped, dead, with keyboard keys stuck in his face. The work lights around the lot continued to strobe. Several blew their bulbs as the lot flashed in and out of darkness like it was the set of a Nine Inch Nails video. It looked rad as hell.

At the intersection, Gina swerved to avoid a fallen power line as Killian reached out with all the power of the glove. She whipped a wrecked cop car into the path of the jeep. Gina pulled hard on the wheel to avoid it.

Killian anticipated her. Gina only had a fraction of a second to react to the car coming at her, flipping end over end. With a flick of Killian's Power Gloved wrist it smashed like a boulder into the side of the jeep. It rolled onto its side and slid along the wet road. B was pinwheeled through the air, hitting the ground with a loud crunch. He lay there, crumpled.

Gina, who was wearing her seat belt like a good girl, hung sideways in the jeep as it slid and then stopped against a lamppost out front of Dock's.

Gina screamed as she saw it coming.

The Goon jeep that was chasing behind them had no time to stop. It plowed into Gina and her jeep. Both vehicles exploded like they were made of gasoline.

From the front of the store, A, C, Annie, Jonathan and Mrs K saw the explosion. Black smoke plumed up from the intersection. They could see fire between the V-Mart vehicles.

C felt her heart sink.

"Was that?' asked A.

"B?" said C.

A shook her face, blank of emotions.

Annie started to sob in heaving breaths.

"WILLIAM!" she screamed.

C walked forward to try and see him. At the rim of the pit, she looked down. Chad Baxter lay on the altar.

"Oh no," said C. She had no time to grieve her friend.

She watched as the The Count slammed the high tech ritual dagger into Chad Baxter's chest.

"We who offer purity and blood," said Augustus and Giles in Latin.

The storm above the V-Mart became a hurricane, a cosmic frenzy of wind and rain.

Chad Baxter gasped as his blood flowed upward through the channels of the dagger. The final golden occult symbol lit up as ultimate power spread through the inlaid veins of gold to the heart of the altar and the symbol lying right below Chad Baxter. The power spidered into inscriptions and symbols on the dagger, which also glowed and pulsed.

Chad Baxter's blood spiraled up into the air, where waiting above a slice of light had appeared. A split. It was a rip in reality. It spread, shooting up in forks like the inverted roots of a tree or lightning which had somehow started from the ground.

It was 9:03.

They'd never stood a chance of running out the clock.

The ritual was complete.

The door was open.

The Great Maw was here.

29

The Great Maw

Killian felt the change in the air and turned to see the rip spread high into the sky and join the swirling storm. Looking back to the lot, she saw The Teeth chasing Goons around. The lights were still pulsating as rain lashed down in sheets. She knew what had happened. Those crusty fucks had finished the ritual. *Her* ritual.

"No. No. NO! THAT'S *MY* RITUAL!"

She power-walked back towards the V-Mart, flicking her glove back and forth to move cars out of the way. A crumpled body lay on the street ahead of her. It was the punk boy who'd been shooting fireworks at her.

At the edge of the pit, everyone else joined C as she looked on helplessly. Chad Baxter's blood continued up and into the darkness beyond the rip that spread above the pit.

The Count knelt in anticipatory supplication.

"They sacrificed Chad Baxter!" C yelled to the others.

"But I mouth sexed him. That counts, right?" said A sobbing.

"Totally," said Annie, still crying for B.

159

"Yes, that counts. Audrey, you can do better," said Mrs K as she tried to calm Cyclops Teeth, who was chattering away. She'd lost control of this situation and she knew it. Her poor Billy, gone.

Head Teeth, Spider Teeth and Horn Teeth gathered with them at the edge of the pit. Cyclops Teeth jumped across to join them, and they spoke their strange Korean dialect to each other. They looked nervous. There was some indecision about their union status.

"They say it's coming," said Annie.

"The Maw," clarified Mrs K. They didn't need clarification.

The rip was massive now, and in the dark beyond the strobing work lights bounced off spinning rows of perfectly white teeth. The Maw's immaculate oral hygiene was just another of this nights confounding mysteries.

On the other side of the pit, a V-Mart van abruptly slid to one side like it was made of nothing to reveal the furious Killian Vass. She was dragging a limp body by its broken arm, and it made sickening noises, like an animal caught in a trap.

A saw Killian and B.

"Look, B's alive!" said A. Annie hugged A, who let it happen. In front of them, just above the pit, were the shimmering limbs of the rip. The light refracted strangely at its edges, creating distortions and a floating reflection that mostly obscured one side of the pit from the other unless you really concentrated.

C burst into tears. She had been holding her shit together all night, but seeing B hurt and alive was too much. Jonathan put a strong hand on her bare back, and she instantly felt better. She realized she was still wearing the stupid sexy Halloween dress, which was now torn in several new places.

Killian reached the top of the scaffold stairs. From her left, scrambling over pieces of a dead Technician came Gap Teeth. It coiled its tiny legs and pounced at Killian's mouth. She dropped B's arm and caught Gap Teeth with her gloved hand. It struggled to get free, snapping at her.

"Cute. Tiff?"

Killian looked around.

"Tiff?' she asked again. Tiffany was cowering behind a computer tape deck. She popped her head up.

"I'm here," she said loudly, to be heard over the storm.

"Let's have marketing dissect this thing and run a focus group on breeding it as a summer promo. Oh, and we'll need to hire a new Gina," said Killian. Tiffany uselessly tried to write in her soaked notebook.

Gap Tooth got a piece of Killian, digging its teeth into her thumb. Killian squeezed it hard with her glove, and Gap Tooth squealed with an ear-piercing shriek before it popped like a balloon of blood and fur.

Across the pit, the other Teeth wailed in pain and gnashed their teeth at Mrs K's feet. Several seemed eager to avenge their union brother.

"Back up! She is too strong," Mrs K said to them in Korean. They stayed put, heeding her warning.

"Everyone, back inside. This is too much. I can open a BBQ place," said Mrs K said to the kids.

C hugged her. "No way. You and this place are all we have. We love you."

A joined the hug, "I have strong feelings."

Annie joined too, "She means she loves you too, and we're not giving up."

They let go, and Mrs K looked at Annie in confusion.

"Who are you?

"She's one of us," said A.

"Aww, babe," said Annie.

"Shut up," said A, looking away.

"Come on. Let's get B," said C. They started walking around the pit towards the top of the stairs.

Killian didn't see them coming. She was busy flicking the gory remains of Gap Teeth off her Power Glove. She reached her other hand into her jacket.

"Umbrella!" she said loudly. Tiffany popped open a V-Mart-branded umbrella and held it over Killian's head. Her hands were shaking. Killian casually pulled out a small vial of white powder, tipped some onto the back of her glove hand and took a big bump. Fur and blood was stuck to her face, but she'd lost the ability to give a fuck about how she looked. She was playing it cool to project calm to her panicked employees, but inside, she raged harder than the storm that surrounded them.

"That's much better," she said, sniffing and rubbing her gums with a slightly blood-stained finger. "Now, what have you crusty old fucks done without me?" she said as she started to descend the stairs.

Down in the pit, The Maw pushed forward. It squeezed through the rip and entered our world mouth-first, its rows of teeth in a lip-less circular grin. Its head was massive, eyeless and covered in dark, wet, matted fur. Its body was still too large to cross through. For now. What could be seen of it was terrifying. It had the shape of a rounded bear like The Teeth, with four clawed limbs. It's body was covered in dried blood-colored plates of bone, like a crab. It had the same black fur everywhere the plates were not.

The Count knelt before the altar. The orbs of the Vass brothers floated at the top of its head. Something occurred to Giles.

"Augustus?"

"Quiet, brother. You'll make it angry again," said Augustus.

Chad Baxter's blood gushed from the dagger, like it was an anti-gravity faucet. The Maw drank from it deeply, like it was Coke Classic on a hot day.

"Are you sure our body man was a virgin?" asked Giles.

"Well, I… Oh no," stammered Augustus.

The Maw roared in displeasure. Its head pushed further out of the rip and it opened its mouth even wider. Its teeth started spinning up.

Still on all fours, The Count started to slowly back away. It kept its head tilted to avoid spillage.

"You have made another classic blunder, Giles! Get ready to run at my nearest convenience," said Augustus.

Reaching the bottom of the stairs, Killian almost stepped on the crawling Count. Tiffany was trying, and failing spectacularly, to hold the V-Mart umbrella over her head, fighting against the combined energy of the storm and the suck of The Maw's vortex.

"It's more beautiful than I ever imagined," said Killian.

"I, Killian Vass the first, welcome you, oh Great Maw," she said in Latin.

The Count was at her feet, and Giles' orb swam around to the back of its head.

"You must kneel. You must show it deference," he begged.

Killian smiled.

"Never. Tiff…"

Tiffany let go of the umbrella which flew away like it was made of paper. She raised her walkie-talkie close to her mouth. "We didn't start the fire."

164

30

Killian's Real Plan

Tiffany's words were broadcast all over the lot. Killian's team within her team, the ones who hadn't panicked at the chaos of the Teeth, were waiting to hear those exact words. They sprang into action.

On the roof of a V-Mart van, a panel running its length depressed with a hiss of gas. It split in two and slid back with a mechanical click crunch clack. A mounted gas powered harpoon gun with a harnessed Goon in a chair popped up. Five identical vans surrounding the pit all did the same thing.

Vehicles and action figures each sold separately.

A hidden panel on the side of the second semi-trailer also opened in the same way. Underneath it, metal stairs unfolded. Inside that semi-trailer were a dozen armored masked V-Mart Goons holding heavily modified shotguns loaded with metal spikes.

Killian's *real* plan had begun.

The harpoon guns fired with a loud bang and popping hiss of pressurized gas and their harpoons flew towards The Maw. Each had a thick heavy chain attached that trailed it. Killian's elite Goons did not miss. They knew where to aim. The harpoons ripped through the fur and thick flesh of The Maw between the hard crab-like plates. They embedded themselves deep in its muscle mass. In the back of the vans, powerful electric motors whirred up as the chains attached to the harpoons reeled in the slack and snapped tight. The Maw lurched forward, being dragged further out of the rip.

The Count stood up.

"What the devil are you doing!?" yelled Giles. Killian walked past him closer to the altar, the rip and her new pet.

"To use an idiom your syphilitic minds might understand, 'Why buy the cow when you can get the milk for free?'" she said.

"I've always said as much but I don't understand its relevance now," said Augustus.

The Maw was furious. It pulled against the chains but they held as its vortex started to lift the corpse of Chad Baxter from the altar.

Meanwhile, at ground level, C reached B first. The others were close behind her. B looked terrible, his face was a mass of cuts and bruises. His left eye was swollen shut. C touched him gently. He groaned and tried to sit up, C helping him.

"I broke my arm," he said, lifting it straight up. It flopped over, limp at the forearm, with a squelching noise. Everyone winced.

"It doesn't hurt," he said. Annie gently grabbed his arm and tried to stop it flopping around.

"Stay still," said C.

"What's that noise?" asked B.

At the rim of the pit, the shotgun Goons fired. Spikes whooshed through the air. Each hit with a hard whomp as they penetrated The Maw's head.

In the pit Killian closed her glove and summoned lightning. She fired it with a crack of thunder and it split into a dozen forks that connected to the spikes.

The Maw convulsed and shuddered as electricity coursed through its body. Its teeth stopped spinning and Chad Baxter's corpse fell back to the altar with a heavy thud. He was still dead. The Maw gagged and coughed, spitting up hyper green colored ooze all over Chad Baxter's body and the altar. It spilled over the edges and ran to the floor.

The Count looked at Killian in awe.

"You would make The Maw *captive!*" said Giles in utter astonishment.

"You are *incredible*," said Augustus, his feelings and tone highly inappropriate for someone who was actually a blood relative of Killian.

Killian walked to the altar and put her hand into the ooze. It was thick and viscous. She played with it between her fingers, like she was a child playing with toy slime.

"Oh, I know. My R&D team have divined that this thing's *'magic'* is merely a side effect of the properties of its sputum. Why bargain with an animal every hundred years when we can keep it here and have constant access to its power by simply stimulating its acid reflux response?" she said in glee.

The Maw reared back, trying to pull itself back to the safety of its realm. The harpoons did not budge. They held it firmly, just where Killian wanted it. Just for fun, Killian shocked it again, closed her eyes, and spread her arms wide. The Maw gagged again and spat out an even bigger stream of ooze. It splattered Killian from head to toe. She was delighted. She turned to The Count. She opened her eyes, lifting her ooze-covered hand and using her long tongue to lick it from wrist to the end of her long delicate index finger.

Killian's stunning green eyes rolled over with hyper green as a film of ooze spread over her entire optic nerve.

"It's gift. Mine. Forever. Want that pony step-mother denied me?" she said.

Instantly Killian was holding the reins of a pure white pony that had not existed a fraction of a second earlier. Her eyes rolled back to their regular green.

"Mine."

The pony shook its mane like a model in a shampoo ad.

"His name is Biscuits," she said.

Biscuits realized the reality of the situation it had been born into and panicked at the sight of The Maw. Killian struggled to hold on to its reins.

Killian quickly tasted the ooze again and her eyes rolled over once more. With a thought, she popped Biscuits out of existence as quickly as he had appeared.

"You get the idea," Killian said as she recomposed herself as much as she could what with her dreams coming true and being totally covered head to toe in demon spit, blood and fur.

"We'll be formulating The Maw's ooze into my own personal Big Suck flavor. Call it 'Cosmic Tonic'. I want it. I suck it. I think it. It's real. It's the power to shape the world to my will," she said.

At her feet, The Count gripped the high tech ritual dagger. Neither of the brothers had realized they were still holding it.

"This is *wrong*," said Augustus.

"Oh really? Tell me so," said Killian with the swagger of a villain whose plan is working and who feels she has all the time in the world to hold court.

"Gus is right for once. This isn't how it is done. The Maw is to be respected," said Giles.

"It's an ancient god that should be free to do god stuff," added Augustus.

Killian laughed at them.

"Oh, fuck off," she said.

"ARE YOU KIDDING ME!?" said C, yelling from the bottom of the scaffold stairs. Behind her were A, B, Annie, Jonathan, Mrs K and The Teeth.

"Ah, the local trouble makers," said Killian looking past The Count and Tiffany, who also turned to see how who was yelling.

"Damn straight we are," said A giving Killian the finger.

"Take your fake pony and get away from my store," said Mrs K.

"You suck," said B.

"Boooooooooo!" said Annie and others joined in.

"I don't like you," added Jonathan.

"Are you *heckling* me?" said Killian, affronted.

"So what if we are?" said C taking a step towards her.

"I could wipe you out of existence without a thought," menaced Killian, pointing to her Power Glove in case they hadn't noticed it.

They laughed at her.

C rolled her eyes. Now that the storm had slowed and The Maw was pacified, she had realized Killian was just another insecure corporate stooge her punk rock idols Henry Rollins of Black Flag and Joe Strummer of The Clash had warned her about. They had trained her for this moment.

"Sure you can, horse girl," said A with all the power of her disdain.

"We don't care about you *or* your pet 'maw'. We just want our curb back, or else," threatened C.

Killian raise an eyebrow, "Or *else?*"

A spun her nunchucks. Annie dodged to not get hit, just as if they'd rehearsed it.

"Just go away, you petty bitch," groaned A.

Tiffany snort laughed. Killian turned on her.

"Did you just *laugh* at me, Tiff?"

Tiffany shrugged and threw her sopping wet notebook to the ground.

"Fuck it. It was funny. I quit. You're the worst," said Tiffany, walking away.

The kids made a hole for her to exit up the stairs. Killian watched her leave in complete utter shock, also horror.

"Brother," whispered Augustus.

"Ready when you are, brother," replied Giles.

The Count ran at Killian.

"I thought we were running *away*," screamed Giles.

"Use our hands. Stab her, brother. Stab her!" yelled Augustus.

The Count raised the high tech dagger to stab Killian but she was too fast. She raised the Power Glove and pulled the dagger from The Count's hand with her magnets. It flew through the air towards her. The Count kept running at her, but Giles lifted its hands in surrender which contradicted Augustus' intention for its legs.

B stepped forward and with his good arm threw the original ritual dagger towards Killian, hoping it would somehow confuse the glove. Killian caught the high tech dagger and stepped out of the way of the charging Count. The original dagger changed direction midair towards Killian's glove. Killian saw it coming and tried to duck out of the way as she simultaneously tried to turn down the glove's power.

The original dagger sliced across her cheek, drawing a line of blood on her perfect complexion. The Count ran into a bookcase lying on its side and flipped head over heels as Giles used its hands to desperately try to stop its liquid spilling out. They were lucky. The Count had flipped all the way round so fast that inertia did them a solid and kept their insides from becoming their outsides.

"NOW YOU ALL *DIE*!" screamed Killian.

She touched her cheek with her the non-gloved hand, bringing back ooze and her own blood. She licked her hand. Her eyes rolled over hyper green. She smiled and gestured dramatically.

Biscuits the Pony popped back into existence beside her and neighed.

"No. I… That wasn't what I wanted to do. I can't stop thinking about that fucking pony," said Killian.

Biscuits panicked and tried to run away. Killian's hands held her reins and had to fight with the whole weight of her body and all her strength not to be dragged away.

Mrs K looked down at The Teeth.

They looked back up. This was their moment, and they knew it. All they needed was an order. Mrs K gave it to them. "Get her," she said in Korean.

The Teeth launched.

A, B, Annie and Jonathan rushed to The Count, who was getting back up.

C went with The Teeth.

Killian dropped Biscuit's reins and reached the Power Glove up into the sky, closing her fist. Lightning cracked down. Before it could reach her the glove powered down with a sad whomp and started beeping. It was out of battery.

The bolt of lightning corrected course. Finding the fastest way to earth, it struck the altar with a tremendous boom. It blasted it apart, along with Chad Baxter's corpse, exploding chunks of marble and senior junior assistant co-manager all over the pit.

Killian was knocked to the ground. Biscuits raced away in terror but couldn't climb the stairs, so it bashed its hoofs uselessly against the walls of the pit, neighing frantically. The Teeth never stopped moving. While everyone else's ears were ringing from the thunderclap and incessant whinnying, and their vision was returning from the lightning flash, The Teeth attacked Killian as she tried to stand up. They knocked her back towards the remains of the altar. Hanging in space above her The Maw was still half in/half out of the rip. It struggled against the harpoons. A chain strained and then snapped. Just that one chain gave The Maw enough slack to move more. It swung its mass up and roared. It pulled so hard against the other harpoon chains that a V-Mart van in the lot hopped and skidded on its tires. It pulled harder in the same direction and the Harpoon Goon barely had time to jump free as the van toppled onto its side, crushing a V-Mart Scientist flat.

It was clear that Killian's plan was falling apart. While some Goons ran, others tried to maintain control of The Maw. A brave and stupid few tried to come down the stairs to Killian's aid but found Mrs K waiting there with her cattle prod. She shocked anyone who got close to her and yelled Korean insults we do not dare publish.

Head Teeth climbed up Killian, trying to reach her mouth. It wanted her teeth. She tried to bite it.

From five feet away C aimed her crossbow at Killian but there was no clear shot with The Teeth all over her.

A smacked The Count in the face with her nunchucks. Its plastic face cracked wide open and liquid poured out of the cartoon vampire's nose.

"Stop! Betrayal! We helped you…" pleaded Augustus.

Annie hit the back of its legs with her baseball bat and they too cracked.

The Count fell to its knees, leaking from top and bottom.

"We'll follow the tenets of Dalton…" said Giles.

From behind, Jonathan wrapped The Count in a bear hug, pining its arms.

"We're good guys now," begged Augustus.

A pulled two packets of Mentos from her cleavage and handed one to B.

"Opinions vary," said B as he ripped open the packet with his teeth. He and A dumped the Mentos candies into The Count's head.

Jonathan let it go.

The Big Suck liquid in the head reacted violently to the Mentos. Big Suck foamed and burst out of its head like a homemade science fair volcano. The brothers screamed as both their orbs blew out of The Count's now wrecked body which cracked all over and clattered to the ground, once again inanimate.

"Science!' yelled A.

She lifted her hand to high five B. He lifted his bad arm and it flopped over.

"It's starting to hurt now," he said.

At their feet the orbs that were Augustus and Giles rolled around like baseball-sized marbles with slightly melted edges.

C dropped the crossbow. She was never going to get a shot off. Looking around for something heavy to hit Killian with instead, she found it.

The *Invocatio Dentium* lay in the debris of the altar. C picked it up and closed distance to Killian as she struggled against The Teeth. C swung the giant tome at Killian, hitting her with a series of solid body shots. Bam bam bam. Her attack gave The Teeth the opening they needed.

Horn Teeth and Cyclops Teeth worked as a tag team to grab Killian's mouth and wrench it open. Head Teeth reached in and tore out two pawfuls of teeth. Killian screamed as blood poured out of her mouth. She was an absolute mess: singed, bleeding from her face and mouth and still slick all over with hyper green Maw spit that was starting to harden like Smucker's Magic Shell. It cracked as she moved and fell off her in chunks.

Killian grabbed Head Teeth and threw it across the library. It bounced off a bookcase and stood up. It jammed the victory teeth into its mouth and chewed them like gum. Cyclops Teeth jumped off Killian and ran to Head Teeth to get its share.

Killian shook off Horn Teeth. It landed on a broken chunk of altar. It bared its teeth and hissed at her through them. It pounced at her and she slashed it with the high tech dagger stuck in the shut down Power Glove.

Horn Teeth fell to the ground screaming. Its adorable tiny intestines spilled onto the ground as it died. Spider Teeth now joined the attack, climbing up Killian's legs and onto her back. Killian ignored it and slashed at C with the dagger. C ducked and then rose up, smacking Killian in the face with the heavy book. C heard Killian's nose crack.

Killian stumbled back, unbalanced at the worst possible moment.

The Maw had been ripping harpoon after harpoon from its body and was now free. It roared so loudly the sound rippled through C's body like a killer bass line. The Maw's teeth began to spin. The suction pulled everything in the pit towards it.

"Get out of there," yelled Mrs K from the stairs as the wind whipped the library into a frenzy of debris, books, dried green slime, dead Teeth and whatever else was lying around.

A and Annie helped B fight the suction and get back to the stairs. Jonathan pushed them from behind, leaning forward and pumping his thick thighs against the suck. He was glad he never skipped leg day. Chad Baxter's headless torso and limbs lifted from the rubble of the altar and into The Maw, the pieces blitzing on The Maw's teeth. What was left was like red rain that spiraled into the wind hitting everyone in the pit.

The power of the wind wrestled the *grimoire* from C's hands. It spun up, spiraling into The Maw's teeth and shredded countless centuries of occult knowledge into instant confetti. The handheld fan that had been used in the ritual clanged around inside The Maw like change that's fallen out of someone's pocket in a washing machine. The original dagger disappeared, whole, straight down its gullet.

The power of The Maw's suction grew even stronger. Killian grabbed a chunk of the altar with her non-gloved hand as her legs lifted from the ground. C tried to run to the stairs but was dragged backwards. She, too, lifted up and flew backwards through the air. With one hand she desperately grabbed the same chunk of altar that Killian was clinging to.

Biscuits. Poor Biscuits. Still stuck in the pit, he tumbled through the air past A and C and well... you know what happened. One last whinny and horsey chunks.

A, B, Annie, Jonathan and Mrs K made it out of the pit seconds before the scaffold stairs ripped apart and joined the storm.

Killian and C ducked their heads to avoid being knocked off their chunk of altar by flying bits of aluminum tubing and a couple of stray horse's hooves. Spider Teeth lost its grip on Killian's back and was pulled into its master's mouth. It burst with a puff of fur and blood as its own teeth pinged off The Maw's.

Head Teeth and Cyclops Teeth each gripped the broken edge of a piece of the marble floor with one paw. In their other paws they now held the orbs of Giles and Augustus. The brothers screamed in terror and begged The Teeth to not let go.

Killian tried to stab C with the high tech ritual dagger still locked in her Power Glove. Her rage knew no bounds. These fucking children had ruined everything! Her life's work amounted to little more than a few precious seconds of pony ownership. She tried to stab C again, but missed as the suction of The Maw threw off her aim.

"Love your nails," said C, meaning it. Killian smiled at her as blood flowed from the holes where her teeth had been.

"Thank you," slurred Killian. "I'm gonna need some dental work after this though, hey?"

C slid her hands along the altar to get closer to Killian. Killian couldn't move. The weight of the glove was an anchor pulling her towards the The Maw and forcing her to use every fiber of her strength to hold on with her other hand.

From the top of the library pit, Mrs K and the kids watched as C put her face next to Killian's and licked hyper green ooze from her face.

It tasted like spearmint battery acid.

C's eyed rolled over hyper green.

Time stopped for C.

Everything went quiet.

She felt her body both in the real world and somewhere else: a hyper green void *between* worlds. She felt a presence there.

The Maw.

She could feel the warmth of its body.

Hear its blood pumping in her ears.

It's breath was *her* breath.

They were connected.

It's rage was a torrent of violence that passed through her soul in a wave.

And beneath that something else.

It was pleased with her.

"We win," said C as time snapped back and she returned from the void. No time had passed out here, but she now stood at the edge of the library pit with her friends, A, B, Annie, Mrs K, and all of The Teeth, somehow even The Teeth that had been killed. Head Teeth held Augustus and Giles' orbs tightly in its paws.

Everything was as she had shaped it to be with The Maw's gift. Back the way it should be, although C had added a few small embellishments.

Jonathan was shirtless and holding a box of Coke Classic.

B waved his unbroken arm. His face was bruise free. He drummed his hands on his chest.

Across the street in the Sizzler, Chad Baxter was ugly scream crying in the empty restaurant remembering how it felt to die.

Gina screamed too. She was alive, lying in the wet grass of the empty lot looking up at the smirking face of the Carpet King. She was going to beauty school and that was that.

In the library pit, The Maw was harpoon free. It roared.

Killian stood alone in front of the spinning vortex of teeth and doom.

"Fucking Biscuits," she muttered a second before she was sucked into The Maw and became a fabulous chunky red mist mixed with atoms of Power Glove.

They all watched as The Maw pulled back into the rip before it stitched itself closed. The storm above the lot evaporated. The sky was once more filled with silent stars.

A, B, and C hugged each other first and then everyone else. B and Annie kissed.

So did C and Jonathan. A rolled her eyes at them.

Mrs K picked up a V-Mart walkie-talkie.

"You assholes have three minutes to leave my property or I let the *dokkaebi* eat your teeth," she said over the RV's PA system.

Head Teeth, standing on her shoulder, roared. Mrs K held up the walkie-talkie and it sounded enormous over the PA. Around the lot, the dozen or so remaining V-Mart Occultists, Scientists and Goons fled as fast as they could.

The Teeth started happily scavenging the teeth from all the bodies that were scattered all around.

It was over.

They had saved their world, and C would still be home before curfew.

31

Six Weeks Later

The Underwood V-Mart looked as good as new. Better, even. Sparkling. The library pit was filled in with concrete and repaved with fresh car park lines on the shiny black tarmac. It was almost Christmas, and the weather in Underwood was actually cold, maybe even threatening to snow.

Inside the store, Mrs K was in her usual spot behind the counter, reading a copy of Convenience Quarterly with a photo of herself on the cover. She was pretty happy with the article, but hated the photo. Next to her on the counter was a large fish tank filled with frozen light blue liquid. Floating in Sour Bubblegum were the orbs of Augustus and Giles. Mrs K had employed The Teeth to watch them and stop them from doing any incantations or invocations. It had taken some time to convince The Teeth of the value of money, but they were now on board.

"Look, brother," said Augustus, his orb floating high in the tank.

On the store's TV, Patrick Swayze was kissing the neck of

Demi Moore as *Unchained Melody* by The Righteous Brothers played.

Giles, miserable, sulked at the bottom of the tank.

"Leave me alone, brother."

"Dalton returns!" said Augustus, clinking excitedly against the glass.

He watched as 'Dalton' and a ruffian scuffled. A gunshot rang out.

Augustus gasped.

Demi Moore held 'Dalton' as he died.

"Oh no," said Augustus.

"Ha. He is dead, like us," said Giles.

Swayze touched his face, and his hand passed through it.

"He's a ghost brother. Mrs K, you must rent us this tape post haste," said Augustus.

Mrs K didn't look up, but she picked up the TV remote and switched it to MTV.

"Don't get any ideas and shoosh, I'm reading," she told them.

"We know you are hiding the art of *Dirty Dancing* from us," said Augustus.

"Blah, blah, blah," Mrs K said, ignoring them.

On MTV, the black and white video for *Can't Hardly Wait* by The Replacements started. B, in a V-Mart uniform, perked up and turned to watch.

"Hell yeah. Turn it up, Mrs K!" he said. She did.

In the aisles, The Teeth stopped mopping with their cut-off mops and started dancing.

"Mrs K, I'm going on break!" B called out as he headed to the front doors.

"Yeah, yeah, whatever. Tell A to pick up her butts," Mrs K

said, busy reading her own press.

Head Teeth popped out of a row of potato chips in front of Jonathan, who dropped the box he was carrying onto his foot. He yelped in pain, and Head Teeth laughed his tiny butt off.

The door dinged and B came out holding a Monster Sized Big Suck and a Classic Coke. He sat on the curb next to Annie, who was sitting in their spot with A and C.

"Mrs K owns the whole *company?*" said Annie, who still couldn't believe it. They had only told her several hundred times.

"She's the only surviving stockholder. Free Big Sucks for life," said A.

Somehow, Vass Enterprises had been able to keep their corporate structure a tontine, which meant that on death a shareholder's stock was redistributed equally among the living shareholders until only one remained, despite this system being outlawed in the early nineteen hundreds. Mrs K's new fancy lawyer had explained it was something to do with the Vass family blackmailing a senator to keep a molasses scandal out of the papers and the grandfathering in of a state law that meant they were able to keep Vass Enterprises from having to operate like a regular public company.

Whatever the hell any of that meant, it was awesome.

B handed C her Big Suck and A her Classic Coke. A hugged it to her face.

"I don't think Chad Baxter is coping with being stabbed in the chest and pulped and then being alive again," said B, pointing.

Chad Baxter stood across the street in the Sizzler car park, staring at A and holding a boom box Lloyd Dobbler in *Say Anything* style above his head. At this distance, they could barely hear Peter Gabriel crooning his 1986 Billboard Mainstream Rock Number 1 hit *In Your Eyes*.

"You still doing secret sports store mouth stuff with him?" asked C.

"No," said A too fast.

"I don't believe you," said B.

"Shut up," said A.

They fell silent for a minute and enjoyed the vibe of the curb.

Even six weeks later, none of them could quite believe what they'd been through.

That they had survived. C had saved the world.

"Do you wish you'd used The Maw's spit magic to do something crazy like make yourself president or rich or Stevie Nicks?" said Annie, asking the question they had all been wondering about endlessly since C had described what had happened when she swallowed The Maw's ooze. Even in the timeless green void she'd only had a fraction of a second to decide how shape the world. She thought she'd done okay, considering.

"Nope. This is exactly what I wanted," C said as she took a massive suck of her Big Suck. Instant brain freeze. Instant regret. She dropped it, and it spilled over the lot.

"Dude!" said B.

"Get me another one, B?" said C, rubbing her head.

"It's my job to clean that now," B said.

"I'll go," said Annie, heading into the store.

The three of them looked at each other. A, B and C, back in *their* spot. They knew it couldn't always be like this. Things would change. They already had. Annie and Jonathan often sat on the curb with them, too now. But right now it was just the three of them, and it was perfect.

A ruined it. That was *still* her thing.

"Hey, what do you guys want to do for New Year's?" she asked.

B and C groaned in unison.

"Nothing," said B.

"Sit quietly," said C.

"Boring," said A.

They all laughed.

"Boring is good," said C.

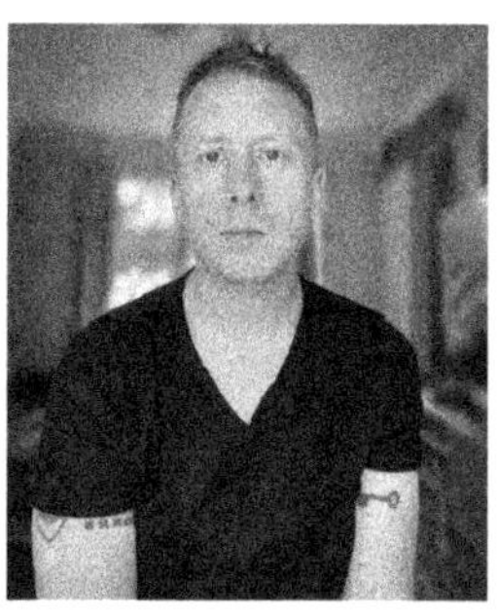

About the Author

Keean Murrell-Snape is an author, filmmaker and podcaster who grew up in the eighties and nineties before the internet ruined everything. He started writing as a teenager after discovering the work of Christopher Pike, to whom he owes an eternal debt of gratitude. *Occult 24/7* is his debut novel, and he hopes you enjoy it so that he can return to the witch in the forest that raised him with good news. You can listen to Keean run his mouth about movies from the golden age of VHS on the *Weird Kid Video Podcast* available on all the podcast things.

9 781764 458009